W9-COI-223

DATE DUE

THE BROKEN ANCHOR

NANCY DREW MYSTERY STORIES®

THE BROKEN ANCHOR

by
Carolyn Keene

Illustrated by
Paul Frame

WANDERER BOOKS
Published by Simon & Schuster, New York

Manufactured in the United States of America
10 9 8 7 6 5 4 3 2 1

NANCY DREW and NANCY DREW MYSTERY STORIES
are trademarks of Stratemeyer Syndicate,
registered in the United States Patent
and Trademark Office

WANDERER and colophon are trademarks of Simon & Schuster

Library of Congress Cataloging in Publication Data

Keene, Carolyn.
The broken anchor.

(Nancy Drew mystery stories; 70)
Summary: A quest for pirate treasure takes clever detective Nancy
Drew and her friends to a small island in the Bahamas.
[1. Mystery and detective stories. 2. Buried treasure—Fiction] I.
Frame, Paul, 1913- ill. II. Title. III. Series: Keene, Carolyn. Nancy
Drew mystery stories; 70.
PZ7.K23   Nan no. 70 [Fic]   82-21947
ISBN 0-671-46462-0
ISBN 0-671-46461-2 (pbk.)

Contents

1

Contest Winner

"Did you enter another contest, Nancy?" Hannah Gruen asked the pretty eighteen-year-old who was eating her lunch.

"Not lately, why?" Nancy smiled up at the Drews' housekeeper.

"This came in the mail." Hannah handed her a large brown envelope.

Nancy stared at it for a moment, seeing the handwritten "Contest Winner" that had been scrawled above the typed name and address.

"Sweet Springs Resort, Anchor Island, Bahamas?" she asked, arching an eyebrow. "I know I didn't enter any contest there."

"Why don't you open it and see what you've won?" Hannah said impatiently.

"You should have been a detective," Nancy teased as she followed her suggestion.

The doorbell rang as she shook out the contents of the envelope, and in a moment Hannah admitted Bess Marvin and George Fayne, Nancy's best friends. "What did you win, Nancy?" Bess asked, seating herself at the table. "Hannah told us about the letter."

"When did you enter a contest?" George asked. Tall and dark-haired, she was quieter than her blond, pretty cousin.

Nancy giggled. "I think it must be a mistake," she answered. "I didn't enter any contest."

"What do they say?" Hannah asked.

Nancy scanned the letter, then handed it to George so she could read it aloud.

"Dear Miss Drew:"

"You have been selected by the Sweet Springs Resort to receive a week-long holiday for two. Your reservations are waiting and airline tickets are enclosed. We can promise you an exotic and beautiful holiday on a very

special island. We will look forward to welcoming you when you arrive in Nassau on Friday.

"Till then, our congratulations, Miss Drew."

George studied it for a moment, then shrugged. "It's signed the owners and staff of Sweet Springs Resort, but no specific names."

"Oh, how exciting," Bess gasped. "When do you leave?"

Nancy handed her the plane tickets. "These are for tomorrow," she answered.

"Do you think it's a legitimate offer, Nancy?" Hannah asked as she brought glasses of iced tea and a plate of sandwiches for the other two girls.

"It could be an advertising gimmick," George suggested. "After all, you and your father are quite well known, Nancy. And this announcement is a bit of a mystery."

"Oh, you must go and see, Nancy," Bess said, giggling. "It would be so romantic to vacation on an island in the Bahamas."

"Well, I don't know," Nancy mused, intrigued by the prospect, yet skeptical of the way it had come about. "I'll have to check into it more carefully, and with Dad gone. . ."

"Where is your father?" George asked, taking the brochure that had come with the letter.

"He was called to Miami early this morning," Nancy answered, leaning over to look at the bright pictures. "I don't know what it was all about."

"This certainly looks like a wonderful place," Hannah observed, studying the brochure. "If the offer is genuine, Nancy, it would be a shame to let it pass."

"How could I find out?" Nancy asked, her gaze on the picture of the elegant pink building with its burgundy tile roof.

"You could call your travel agent and see if the place is for real," George suggested.

"And I suppose the airline could tell me about the tickets," Nancy agreed, getting to her feet, lunch now forgotten.

"I don't know how she can bear to even ask questions," Bess said, munching a sandwich as she studied the photograph of a white sand beach dotted with sunbathers. "I'd just start packing and worry about the details later."

George shook her head. "This is the off-season down there, isn't it?" she asked no one in particular. "I thought most of these places closed at the end of May." She scanned the descriptive paragraphs quickly.

"Does it say they're closed?" Bess asked.

"No dates at all," George reported, her fingers ruffling her hair. "Just a lot of words about beautiful beaches, boat trips, swimming, fishing, things like that."

Bess moaned. "Why don't we ever get wonderful surprises like this?"

"I guess. . ." George stopped as Nancy came back into the kitchen. "What did you find out?"

Nancy kept her expression solemn for a moment, but then she could bear it no longer and grinned at her two friends. "It seems to be genuine," she answered. "The plane tickets are confirmed all the way to Nassau, and though this is a bit late for a vacation in the Bahamas, the travel agent says the Sweet Springs Resort has a good reputation. He suggested that it might be a promotional offer."

"So are you going?" Bess asked eagerly.

"I won't know till I talk to Dad," Nancy replied.

"Can't you call him?" Hannah asked.

Nancy shook her head. "He didn't know where he could be reached when he left. He should be calling me pretty soon, though."

The girls returned their attention to the luncheon that Hannah had provided, discussing the clothes that Nancy should take and the possibilities of her finding a mystery to solve once she arrived on Anchor Island. They'd progressed to ice cream and brownies when the telephone rang.

"I'll get it, Hannah," Nancy called, leaping to her feet and hurrying into the office.

"Hi, honey," her father replied to her greeting. "How are things on the home front?"

"Busy and confusing," Nancy answered.

"Oh, has something happened?" There was concern in Carson Drew's tone.

"Something nice, I think," Nancy replied, then explained about the holiday she'd been offered, finishing, "The only bad part about it is that the plane tickets are for tomorrow and I don't suppose they can be changed."

"How do Bess and George feel about the trip?" Carson asked, surprising her.

"They think we should go." Nancy hesitated, then continued, "What do you think, Dad? Will your business allow you to leave tomorrow?"

"I'm afraid neither one of us can leave that soon, honey. I'm going to need you here," her father said. "However, I do have a suggestion.

"Why don't you let Bess and George take the plane tickets and the reservations for the resort?

You can all fly to Miami tomorrow, and they can go on to the island and make reservations for us to join them as soon as we're finished here."

"Oh, Dad, that would be wonderful," Nancy gasped. "I know they'd love the chance to visit the island—but do you think it will be all right with the resort people?"

Her father laughed. "Since they offered the reservation free, I'm sure they will be happy to have two paying guests in addition. However, if there is any problem, George or Bess can call us when they get to the resort."

"Now tell me about the case you're on," Nancy said, her curiosity aroused as she realized that her father hadn't mentioned anything beyond the fact that he wanted her to come to Miami. "Is there something I can help you with?"

"There certainly is," he replied. "In fact, that's why I'm calling. I've been summoned down here to investigate a real mystery."

"What kind of mystery?" Nancy was intrigued.

"Well, when the authorities contacted me, they said that it was about an abandoned boat. They think I can identify the owners."

14

"Can you?" Nancy asked when he hesitated for several seconds.

"I haven't actually seen the boat yet," he continued. "It's up the coast from Miami, and this morning they seemed more anxious to ask me questions about my background and about you. In fact, they'd like you to join me."

"Me, why?"

"Well, according to the sheriff, the boat had been stripped of any identification before it was abandoned. In fact, the only clue that they found on board was a file of newspaper clippings."

"Newspaper clippings?"

"All concerning cases where you've helped me solve mysteries," her father explained.

"Then the owners of the boat were interested in us?" Nancy frowned. "That makes two mysteries today."

"Two?"

"Well, I don't know how I could win a contest that I didn't enter, and now we seem to have fans who've disappeared off their boat."

"Do you think you can arrange to get down here tomorrow morning?" her father asked. "What flight are those tickets for?"

Nancy got the tickets and gave her father the information, adding that she'd already inquired about another seat being available, since she'd hoped that Bess and George would be able to accompany her, if her father couldn't. He laughed at her words. "Always one step ahead of me, aren't you?" he teased.

"Just trying to be a good, efficient daughter," Nancy answered with a giggle.

"Efficient enough to locate the owners of the abandoned boat, I hope," he told her. "We'll have to solve that mystery before we can go on to the resort to find out why they've been so generous to you." He hesitated, then added, "You are sure that you didn't enter some contest or drawing or something?"

Nancy laughed. "I'd never forget a contest that had a prize like this, Dad. Just wait till you see the brochure. It really looks like a fantastic place for a vacation. Our travel agent said that it's normally booked full during the winter season, so I doubt that this is a promotion to get new customers or advertising."

"Then what is it?" her father asked.

"A mystery," was the only answer she could give him.

2

Mystery Boat

Bess and George were delighted with Carson Drew's suggestion. After a series of phone calls and a busy planning session, the three girls split up to make their preparations for the next day's early flight. Hannah came up to help Nancy with her packing.

"Is something wrong, Nancy?" she asked as she folded an array of summer clothes.

"I just keep wondering why my name was chosen for the holiday," she admitted. "I know it wasn't a contest and I don't think it was advertising, so why?"

"People have heard of you," Hannah reminded her. "It's like that file on the boat that your father told you about. Maybe the people at

17

the resort just wanted to meet you and thought that this was a good way to extend an invitation."

Nancy smiled. "Won't they be surprised when they meet Bess and George instead?"

"Perhaps you and your father will be able to solve the mystery in Florida very quickly," Hannah said. "Then you can ask the owners of the resort for an explanation."

"I certainly intend to do that," Nancy stated firmly as she added a beach coverup and thongs to the pile of things to be packed.

The flight to Miami proved smooth and uneventful, though Nancy felt a pang of regret as she bid George and Bess farewell. "Now you call us at the hotel after you reach the resort," she told them, giving George the number her father had provided the day before.

"Just get the mystery here solved quickly, so you can join us," Bess said. "It really won't be the same without you, you know." Her pretty face showed her apprehension.

Nancy laughed fondly. "You can still stroll on the moonlit beach and swim in that lovely water," she reminded her.

Carson Drew and Nancy watched till the flight for Nassau took off. Then he took her arm.

"I guess we'd better be on our way, Nancy," he said, his pleasant expression changing to one of concern. "The sheriff is an impatient and unreasonable man, and he is most anxious to have you examine this boat."

"Is there more to this than you've told me, Dad?" Nancy asked, her own mystery forgotten now. "You seem troubled."

"I just don't like being suspected of something," her father replied. "The sheriff hasn't been able to find out anything about the boat, and he seems to think that I'm hiding something from him."

"Well, maybe we can find a clue today," Nancy consoled him. "Something the sheriff has missed. Where exactly did they find the boat?"

"It was located by a couple of young boys fishing along a deserted inlet," her father explained as they got into the rental car. "It's a big powerboat, the kind that does quite well on the ocean traveling between islands. That's why the sheriff is having so much difficulty finding the owners. Many of the people on the islands seem to have similar boats, and with all the identification removed, he's having to wade through all the missing-boat reports from the United States and various island groups."

"You mean it could have come here from somewhere else?" Nancy asked.

Her father nodded. "From a Caribbean Island or from the Bahamas—or from anywhere in this area."

"Where are we going now?" Nancy inquired, enjoying the passing scene.

"I thought we'd drop your luggage off at the hotel, then drive up to Palm Cove. That's the town closest to the inlet. We went in by helicopter yesterday, so the sheriff said he'd leave a map with his deputy and meet us on the boat. How does that sound?"

"Lovely," Nancy answered. "How far is it?"

"Should be about an hour's drive to Palm Cove. Beyond that, I'm not sure."

Since most of the highway took them along the coast, the drive proved to be very beautiful, giving views of the beaches and the water as it washed sand or rocks. June had brought to the area a richness of flowers and thick-growing plants that made it a tropical paradise quite different from River Heights.

It was nearing noon by the time they reached Palm Cove, so they stopped for lunch at an old-fashioned seafood restaurant before going to the sheriff's office.

"Doesn't look like a very lively town, does it," Carson Drew observed as they watched three sleepy-looking dogs make their way across the nearly deserted main street.

Nancy giggled. "I'm sure any strangers would be noticed." They ordered their food, then looked out over the little cove that had given the town its name.

Nancy's observation proved quite correct, for a uniformed young man came up to their table before they'd finished their meal. "Mr. Carson Drew?" he asked politely.

Mr. Drew nodded. "May I help you?"

"The sheriff asked me to give this to you," the deputy said. "I saw you drive up over here, so I thought I'd save you the trip to the office." His admiring gaze touched Nancy, then dropped. "The sheriff is anxious to have your daughter look at the boat."

"Has there been any progress in locating the owners?" Mr. Drew asked, inviting the young man to join them.

"You'll have to ask Sheriff Boyd about that, sir," the deputy replied, then began to explain the rough map he'd brought. Nancy and her father finished eating while he spoke, then they all left.

Though the last few miles of the trip were made over back roads that were still rutted from the spring rains, Nancy and her father had no difficulty following the map to the tree-draped inlet. Once there, they found the sheriff's dusty cruiser parked beside an age-grayed, half-rotted dock. The boat had been neatly tied to the strongest of the dock posts.

Sheriff Boyd, a beefy man in his forties with dark brown hair and angry brown eyes, came out on the deck as soon as he heard their car. "It's about time you got here," he greeted them, his expression reflecting his frustration. "Do you recognize the boat, girl?"

Nancy looked at her father but could read nothing in his handsome face, so she joined him as they walked out on the dock and stepped aboard. The boat deck showed excellent care, but it was already spotted with fallen leaves from the trees that sheltered it.

"Well?" the sheriff prompted after Carson introduced Nancy.

"I've never seen this boat, Sheriff," Nancy stated firmly.

"Nor have I," Carson Drew echoed her. "As I told you yesterday."

The sheriff's frown deepened as he led them

into the cabin that opened off the deck. "Then how do you explain this?" he asked, handing Nancy a manila folder.

She opened it. There were a half-dozen clippings in a variety of newsprints, indicating that they had come from at least two or possibly three different newspapers. They covered cases from the past year and were all glowing reports of Nancy's exploits as a detective.

"Anything occur to you, Nancy?" her father asked as he scanned the reports.

Nancy shook her head. "I don't see any connection between the cases," she answered. "And they are all from different areas, so it can't have anything to do with this or any other particular location."

"But they were found on this boat," Sheriff Boyd protested.

Nancy handed the file back to the sheriff. "The people who own it must have been interested in my father's career or mine, but that doesn't mean that we know them. These could have been clipped from any newspapers that carried the stories. Unless they contacted us about something . . ." She let it trail off.

Sheriff Boyd sighed. "That's exactly what your father said," he admitted.

"You've learned nothing more about the boat?" Carson Drew asked.

"We do have a tentative name," the sheriff answered. "I traced one of the appliances in the galley to a Miami store. The names of the purchasers were Jeff and Lena DeFoe. Do those names mean anything to you?"

"DeFoe?" Carson's eyes sought Nancy's.

She concentrated, then shook her head. "I don't think I've ever heard the name," she said. "Is it someone from one of your cases, Dad?"

"Not that I recall," he answered. "I'm sorry, Sheriff Boyd. It just doesn't mean a thing to me. Is there anything else?"

Sheriff Boyd shook his head. "Not so far. However, I'd appreciate it if you'd look around the boat now that we've finished fingerprinting. I'll go check with my deputy and see if he's gotten any further information."

Nancy waited until the sheriff was off the boat, then turned to her father. "What do you think, Dad?" she asked.

"Let's see if the sheriff missed anything," he suggested. "Where do you want to start?"

"In here, I guess." Nancy went to the enclosed shelves to look at the small collection of dishes stored there.

24

"Mr. Drew." Sheriff Boyd's call summoned her father out on deck while Nancy continued to open drawers and look into cubbyholes around the cabin. She was just about to go down into the lower cabins when her father returned.

"Did he have any more information?" she asked, noting her father's strange expression.

"His deputy just radioed the news that Jeff and Lena DeFoe are owners of a resort in the Bahamas. They don't have the name of it yet, but it's located on Anchor Island."

Nancy gasped. "But that's where Sweet Springs Resort is located. Didn't I tell you that?"

He shook his head.

"Oh, Dad, Bess and George are on their way there now," Nancy groaned. "What do you suppose is going on?"

3

An Ancient Clue

For several minutes neither of them spoke, then Nancy shook off the sudden chill her words had brought. "Should we tell Sheriff Boyd?" she asked. "About the contest and the island, I mean."

"Of course," her father answered, "but I'm afraid it will have to wait. He got a radio call while we were talking and had to leave. He said if we found anything we should stop by his office on our way back to Miami. We can tell him then, I suppose."

"But what about Bess and George?" Nancy asked, terribly worried about her two friends.

"There's nothing we can do till they reach the resort," her father answered. "They've already landed in Nassau, and they should be on their way to the resort by now. Let's finish searching the boat. If there is a connection between it and that mysterious contest you didn't enter . . ." He didn't have to finish.

Nancy took a deep breath and nodded. "You think the DeFoes sent that intriguing prize to me?" she asked.

"If they did compile that file of clippings, they would know that you'd be likely to accept such an invitation," her father reminded her.

"But they could have simply called. Why do you suppose they want me to go to Anchor Island?"

Her father could only shrug. "Perhaps we'll get some real answers when Bess and George call tonight," he suggested.

"And till then we'll just go ahead with our search of the boat," Nancy said.

"Did you finish in here?" her father asked.

She nodded.

"Well, I'll go up and look around the bridge while you tackle the cabins below," he told her.

Nancy stepped through the doorway and down the few stairs to the lower level of the boat. Three doors opened off the small landing. One led into a little bathroom, the other two gave access to small, neat cabins that appeared to be exactly alike.

Nancy stepped into the cabin on her right first. Twin bunks were freshly made up. There were a few clothes hanging in the tidy closet, but the pockets of both shirts and slacks were disappointingly empty. The built-in dressing table yielded little more in the way of clues.

A hairbrush with a few light hairs in it, an old pink lipstick, several battered knit tops, and a stained old fisherman-knit sweater were all she could find. Even taking out each drawer to inspect the bottom and the space it had filled yielded nothing. Just to be on the safe side, Nancy stripped, then remade each bunk.

Her inspection of the other cabin proved unenlightening, for it held nothing personal. Nancy searched it as carefully as she had the first cabin but with even less success.

Frustrated, she searched the small bath, finding further traces of the DeFoes, but nothing else. She hesitated at the foot of the steps, sure that there was nowhere else to search, yet feeling that she shouldn't give up so easily.

"What happened to you folks?" she asked the warm silence of the cabin. "Why did you send me an invitation you knew I couldn't resist,

28

then come all the way to Florida to disappear?"

The boat creaked and moved slightly on the lazy swelling of the inlet. Nancy crossed to one of the bunks and started to bend down to reach across it to run her fingers along the shadowy area where the bunk rested against the wall, seeking a break or crevice. As she did so, the boat shifted again and she stumbled slightly, bumping the side of her face against the wall.

The silence was broken by a click and a rolling sound. Nancy lifted her hand to her ear, realizing at once that she'd lost her earring. She looked down just in time to see her earring disappear into a dark corner.

"Oh, dear" she muttered, dropping to her knees to pursue it. "Come back here."

Her fingers grated on wood without finding the familiar shape of her earring. Frowning, she probed the area and then gasped as her finger slipped into a small hole. It went in easily, not encountering anything below. When she tried to pull it back out, the whole section of wood in the corner caught on her knuckle and lifted out.

"Well, well, well," Nancy murmured, looking at the square of wood in her hand.

The area it opened was not large, but her earring lay on top of an old leather pouch. Nancy lifted them both out carefully, then peered into the small recess to make sure there was nothing else hidden there. Convinced that it was empty, she replaced the wooden tile and put her earring on before opening the pouch.

"Find something?" Her father's voice made her start and she nearly dropped the heavy medallion that slid out of the pouch when she released the thong that held it shut.

"I think so," Nancy answered, explaining quickly what had happened to her earring.

Her father whistled as he held up the medallion. "This looks like pure gold, Nancy," he said.

Nancy got to her feet and followed him to the small porthole which gave the cabin daylight. The three-inch disk fit into her palm, but its surface was so dirty and scarred she couldn't make out the design in the metal.

"It looks very old, Dad," she observed, rubbing at the surface.

Carson Drew nodded. "The workmanship on the chain is definitely ancient, and the disk itself is beautifully shaped. Too bad it's so battered."

"It looks like some kind of hook or something," Nancy said. Perhaps someone familiar with antique jewelry could tell us what it's supposed to be."

Her father's eyes lit up. "I know just the man," he said. "Do you remember Avery Yates?"

Nancy thought for a moment. "The jeweler who specializes in restoring antique jewelry?"

"That's the one. He retired to this area a couple of years ago. I think I have his phone number in my things at the hotel."

"Could we take it to him tonight?" Nancy asked, intrigued by the unusual necklace. "It might be a clue."

Mr. Drew's smile faded. "I'm not sure Sheriff Boyd will be happy about that," he observed.

Nancy's eyes met her father's. "Sheriff Boyd didn't find it," she reminded him.

Her father looked disapproving for a moment, then shrugged. "We'll tell him as soon as Avery finishes with it," he decided. "After all, if we give it to the sheriff now, he probably wouldn't have it restored, so we wouldn't be able to find out what it means."

Nancy hugged him. "Let's hurry back to the hotel," she suggested. "I want to see if Bess and George have called yet."

"We should tell the sheriff about the resort," her father murmured.

"We'll probably know a great deal more after we talk to the girls," Nancy said.

He nodded. "You didn't find anything else?"

Nancy shook her head. "How about you?"

"The sheriff was right about the boat being stripped of identification. The log is gone, the various identification names and numbers have been sanded off or removed. The best I can tell you is that someone, probably Mr. DeFoe, smokes a pipe."

Nancy sighed, then took the medallion and studied it once again. "This must mean something," she told him. "That's why someone had to hide it down there."

"Ready to go?"

"I guess we might as well," Nancy agreed. "There really isn't any place else to search, is there?"

"I'll lock up," her father said, "though I can't imagine many people come out this way."

Nancy went out on the deck and looked around, realizing again just how deserted this area was. The water lapped lazily at the dock pilings, and a breeze stirred the palms and the other trees that shaded the inlet.

"Where could they have gone?" she asked her father, not really expecting an answer.

"Someone must have met them," her father answered, following her line of thinking. "That was one of the things the sheriff kept saying. That inlet is really a strange place to abandon a boat because you can't just walk away from it."

The drive back to the hotel seemed endless to Nancy as she alternately stared at the medallion and worried about her friends. They hurried to the desk to ask for messages.

"Nothing Mr. Drew, Miss Drew," the desk clerk informed them.

"We'll call the resort," her father told her. "Let's go up to our rooms."

Placing the call to Anchor Island proved to be a long, frustrating process, though the hotel switchboard operator was both competent and experienced. It was almost an hour before the phone rang. Nancy hurried to answer it.

"Miss Drew?" Her heart dropped as she recognized the operator's voice once again.

"Did you reach them, Operator?" she asked.

"I'm afraid not. The connection has gone through twice, but there is simply no answer at the resort. Would you like me to keep trying?"

Nancy relayed the information to her father, then handed him the receiver, listening as he cancelled the call, saying they would place it again later. His face was serious when he replaced the receiver.

"Where are Bess and George?" she asked him.

He shook his head. "I wish I knew."

4

Galleon Gold

"What are we going to do?" Nancy asked.

"Well, there really isn't anything we can do to reach the island at the moment," her father said. "So why don't I call Avery and see if we can take the medallion over to him?"

"But—" Nancy began.

"Honey, it is possible that your holiday was to be a private one. I mean, if we're correct in assuming that the same people sent the tickets who collected that file of clippings, they probably wanted you and me to be their only guests."

Nancy frowned. "I can understand that, but why aren't they answering their phone?"

"Perhaps they've let their staff go for the summer and are shorthanded. Maybe they're still en route from Nassau to the island."

"You think that Bess and George are safe?"

"Of course. Now, why don't you relax for a few minutes? You must be tired after having left home so early this morning."

Nancy went obediently to lie on the bed in her room, but she could hear her father's voice through the connecting door. He had no trouble reaching Mr. Yates, who obviously welcomed the call.

In a moment Mr. Drew came to the door. "Avery has invited us to his place for dinner," he said.

Nancy sat up, nibbling at her lip. "I'd love to see him, but what about Bess and George?" she asked. "They're supposed to call."

"Then, I'll invite him to the hotel. They have a very nice rooftop dining room here, and we can leave word with the switchboard so we can be called there or here."

"Thanks, Dad." Nancy lay back again.

Nancy took her time, had a bubblebath, then donned a deep coral dress that set off her fair skin and pretty eyes perfectly. She brushed her hair into curving radiance, using a couple of golden combs to secure it, then smiled at her reflection in the mirror.

Her father came into her room just as she finished. "Avery is downstairs," he said. "I've asked him to come up and see the medallion before we go to the restaurant."

"If only it could tell us something," Nancy said, as a knock on the door announced Mr. Yates's arrival.

Mr. Yates looked just as she'd remembered him: a tall, slim man scarcely stooped by his seventy-five years, his blue eyes as bright and curious as ever. "Miss Nancy, you get prettier every time I see you," he told her as he took her hand. "Quite a young lady now, but still solving mysteries, I hear."

Nancy colored slightly. "I just hope we'll be able to solve this latest one," she said. Then she and her father told the elderly gentleman everything that had happened since the phone call about the abandoned boat and the arrival of the mysterious contest prize.

Mr. Yates listened attentively, shaking his head at the news that they'd been unable to reach anyone on Anchor Island.

"This is what Nancy found under the floorboards of the cabin," Mr. Drew finished, opening the worn leather pouch and letting the medallion drop into Mr. Yates's gnarled hands.

"Oh, my," he breathed, touching the glowing metal with gentle fingers. He lifted it, studying both the medallion and the hand-wrought chain from which it was suspended. "This is quite a find, Miss Nancy, quite a find, indeed."

"Do you think it's pure gold?" Nancy asked.

"Very likely," he replied. "But more than that, I think you have here a genuine piece of history." He moved closer to the lamp, studying the medallion's scarred face. "I'll have to do some work to bring out whatever has been engraved on this disk, but just seeing it, I'd say it's Spanish treasure," Mr. Yates said. "I've examined a number of pieces dating from the days when the galleons plied these waters, and this compares quite favorably with them."

"Spanish gold," Carson Drew murmured.

"Pirate treasure?" Nancy asked.

Mr. Yates nodded to both suggestions. "Either or both," he answered.

"But what does it mean?" Nancy asked. "Can it help us find out what happened to George and Bess and the DeFoes?"

Mr. Yates just shook his head.

"I think we should go up to dinner," Carson Drew suggested. "I'm starving."

Dinner was excellent and the night view of

the ocean and the resort-spangled beach stretched out below them was spectacular, but Nancy found it hard to enjoy any of it. She kept watching the time, her mind on Bess and George. Where could they be? Why hadn't they called to say they had arrived safely? She was almost glad when her father suggested that they return to their room for further visiting.

Mr. Yates stayed only a little while longer, getting to his feet with a sigh. "I will be delighted to restore your find," he told them. "Shall I call you when it's ready?"

Carson nodded. "I'll let you know if we're leaving Miami," he said. "We'll have to get together before that."

"Next time you must come to my home," Mr. Yates told them.

"We'd be honored," Mr. Drew assured him. "And we'll be grateful if you can tell us anything about the medallion, anything at all."

Once the door was closed behind Mr. Yates, Mr. Drew went immediately to the phone and called the hotel operator. Nancy listened to the conversation with a sinking heart. Her father turned to her after he replaced the receiver.

"Nothing at all?" she asked.

He shook his head. "I told her to keep trying all night if necessary."

"Maybe we should call the airport in Nassau," Nancy suggested.

"If no one had met them, the girls would have called us from there," her father noted.

"But where can they be?" Nancy almost wailed. "If anything has happened to them, it will be all my fault."

"Now, now," her father soothed, "let's just wait till morning. Perhaps they'll call then and have some perfectly logical explanation."

Nancy nodded her agreement, but she found it very hard to believe. She went to bed with a heavy heart, desperately worried about her missing friends. Fortunately, she was so exhausted by her day that she slept at once, deeply and without dreams.

The ringing of the phone woke her and she stumbled out of bed, pulling on her robe as she hurried into her father's room. He was just hanging up the phone as she turned on the light.

Mr. Drew shook his head. "That was the sheriff," he answered grimly. "He's on his way over here and he sounded furious."

5

Vanished

"But what—?" Nancy began.

"He didn't say," her father answered. "But I think we'd better get dressed in a hurry. He's on his way over."

They were just finishing a hasty breakfast ordered from room service when a pounding on the door announced that they had a visitor. Carson Drew admitted Sheriff Boyd.

Anger blazed from his dark eyes. He glared first at Carson Drew, then turned to Nancy. "Where is it?" he demanded.

Nancy winced with guilt, her mind filled with images of the medallion.

"Just what is it you're looking for, Sheriff Boyd?" Mr. Drew asked, his voice calm.

"The boat, of course!" Sheriff Boyd snapped. "It's gone. I drove out there this morning and there's not a sign of it."

"Sheriff Boyd, I can assure you that the boat was still tied up at the dock when Nancy and I left," Mr. Drew began. "I locked it up as you requested."

The dark eyes probed him, then turned back to Nancy. "Is that your story, too?" he asked.

"That's the truth, Sheriff," Nancy answered, her cheeks glowing pink at the implication of his question.

"You were the last ones on board," Sheriff Boyd growled.

"Which is an excellent reason why we wouldn't take it," Mr. Drew stated. "Since you knew we were there, it would be foolish for us to steal the boat, wouldn't it?"

Sheriff Boyd stood glowering for a moment, then seemed to wilt.

"Who else knew that it was out there, Sheriff?" Nancy asked.

"I expect half the population of Palm Cove knew," he admitted with a sigh. "We don't have many secrets in a town that size."

"Could it be someone from the town?" Carson Drew asked.

"I don't think so," Sheriff Boyd answered. "They wouldn't be able to use it or sell it without someone finding out, and they'd know I'd be after them if I did find out."

"Perhaps the DeFoes returned for it," Nancy suggested hopefully.

"Not likely," the sheriff answered. "I found out that they run a place called the Sweet Springs Resort, and I've been trying to reach someone there all night without any luck. I'm beginning to think there might be trouble out there and the boat here was just someone's effort to escape."

Nancy swallowed hard, meeting her father's gaze fearfully.

"We've been worried about that, too, Sheriff," Mr. Drew began, then told him the whole story of the prize and the fact that Bess and George hadn't called them. The sheriff's expression grew stormy.

"Why didn't you tell me all this before?" he demanded. "I thought you said you didn't know anything about these people."

"We didn't," Nancy answered. "The prize offer didn't carry the owners' names and I didn't tell my father the name of the island, so he had no way of knowing it was the same place. You were gone before he told me."

"You could have left word at the office." The sheriff looked very suspicious.

Nancy looked at her father, wondering if he was going to mention the medallion. She felt that they should, but the sheriff's suspicious attitude made her sure that it would cause trouble not only for them, but for Mr. Yates, too.

"We were anxious to get back to the hotel to call the girls," Mr. Drew replied. "I thought they would be able to give us valuable information about the DeFoes and the resort. I planned to call you as soon as I talked to them."

"Sure you did." Sheriff Boyd sneered.

"I assure you, Sheriff, I had no intention of keeping information from you," Carson Drew continued. "I've been trying to reach Anchor Island, too. We're very worried about those two young ladies."

"I'm more concerned about what happened to the boat," the sheriff snapped. "I want you to come to my office and make a statement about where you went after you left it yesterday."

"Really, Sheriff," Carson Drew began, a touch of anger showing in his voice.

"A full statement of your movements," the

44

sheriff growled. "And I want it before noon."

The sheriff left before they could offer any further argument. Nancy sighed. "What are we going to do, Dad?" she asked. "About the medallion, I mean."

Her father gave her a wry grin. "I guess we should have told him sooner," he observed. "If we mention it now, he's going to have us both arrested, and we can't help George and Bess from a Florida jail."

"But we didn't do anything wrong," Nancy protested.

"I don't think Sheriff Boyd is in any mood to listen to logical explanations," her father said.

"But we'll have to tell the sheriff we saw Mr. Yates," Nancy began.

"I'll call him and ask him not to mention the medallion. He's simply an old friend who joined us for dinner last night."

"Meantime, we ought to call Nassau and see if we can get a search started," Nancy said. "If we can convince Sheriff Boyd that we had nothing to do with the disappearance of the boat, we should go to Anchor Island ourselves and find out what is going on."

"The sooner the better," her father agreed.

The phone interrupted him. She answered it immediately.

"Miss Drew," the operator said, "I have your call from Anchor Island."

"Oh, at last!" Nancy was overjoyed.

"Go ahead, please."

"Sweet Springs Resort," a male voice announced.

"Hello," Nancy said. "May I speak to George Fayne or Bess Marvin please?"

"What?" The voice was not friendly.

"I would like to speak to one of your guests," Nancy began again. "Miss George Fayne or Miss Bess Marvin. They would have checked in yesterday."

"There's no one here by those names."

"But they had reservations."

Her father touched her arm to get her attention. "In your name, honey," he whispered.

"The reservations were in the name of Nancy Drew," Nancy went on.

"You must have the wrong resort, ma'am," the bland voice went on.

"Is there someone else there I could speak with?" Nancy asked desperately. "Someone in the reservations department or something?"

"There's no one at all here for you to talk to," the voice stated. "Fact is, the resort is closed. I'm the caretaker."

"But—" Nancy began, then stopped as the line went dead.

6

Missing!

"What is it, Nancy?" her father asked, taking the receiver from her cold and shaking fingers.

"He . . . he said that the resort is closed," Nancy gasped. "He said there's no one there but him!"

"What?" Her father's eyes met hers, but offered no answers. "Let me make some phone calls, after which I'm going to have another talk with Sheriff Boyd."

Nancy nodded, sinking into the nearest chair, her worry and frustration paralyzing. She needed action—she wanted to be on her way to Nassau or Anchor Island, not sitting in a hotel room.

Her father's first call went to Avery Yates,

warning him that he would hear from the angry sheriff soon. After he told of their early morning visitor, his voice changed as he said, "Oh, really? That's wonderful. Sounds intriguing. How soon? Terrific, just give us a call."

As soon as he replaced the receiver, he turned to Nancy. "Avery says he worked on the medallion most of the night. He's convinced that it is definitely from the time of the Spanish galleons."

"Has he been able to make out what is engraved in the gold?" Nancy asked.

"He's still working on it, but he thinks he'll finish it some time today."

"Wonderful." Nancy sighed.

"I'm going to call Nassau now," her father said. "Someone at the airport there might know something about what happened to the girls."

It was almost an hour before her father finally slammed the receiver down in frustration. "If one more person tells me they'll get back to me when they have some information, I'm going to make them eat the telephone," he growled.

Nancy sighed, then looked at her watch. "If we're going to drive to Palm Cove before noon, we should leave pretty soon," she warned him.

Her father looked for a moment as though

he'd like to refuse to make the drive. "I don't suppose we'll be able to leave till we talk to the man, so we might as well get it over with."

"Do you think he'll let us go to Anchor Island?" Nancy asked.

"He has absolutely no reason to keep us here," her father stated. "He asked me to investigate the abandoned boat, which I did. I had nothing to do with its disappearance and I'm sure he'll realize that."

"He was so angry this morning," Nancy murmured.

"Well, once he realizes that we may be able to learn something important by going to Anchor Island, I'm sure he'll be happy to let us go."

"I hope you're right," Nancy sniffed.

The trip to Palm Cove was uneventful, and when they reached the sheriff's office, they were treated politely as they made their brief statements about the boat and their activities afterwards. Only when Nancy mentioned the caretaker at the Sweet Springs Resort did the sheriff seem truly interested.

"Did you ask to speak to the DeFoes?" he inquired.

"I asked to speak to someone in authority,"

Nancy replied. "But he said no one was there. The resort was closed."

"Did you believe him?" The sheriff's question startled her.

"Well . . . I . . ." Nancy gulped. "I wanted to ask him more questions, but he hung up."

"That's why we'd like to charter a seaplane and fly to the island this afternoon," Mr. Drew said. "I've instituted a search of the Nassau airport area for the two girls, but I definitely feel we have to check the island ourselves."

Sheriff Boyd stared at them coldly, his gaze telling Nancy that he still felt they were keeping something from him—which made her feel guilty. "And the DeFoes?" he asked.

"We would do everything we could to locate them, too," Mr. Drew said. "I have no idea what is going on but I do feel that it is all connected through that phony prize that was sent to Nancy—the prize that Bess and George were claiming when they disappeared."

Sheriff Boyd nodded. "I'll want to know what you find," he warned. "Especially if you can learn anything about that boat."

"We'll definitely keep you informed," Mr. Drew promised.

"You'll be leaving today?"

"That depends on how quickly I can make the arrangements," Carson Drew replied. "And what I learn from my calls to Nassau."

"Let me know before you leave," Sheriff Boyd ordered, then dismissed them.

"Do you want to have lunch at the same place?" her father asked as they stepped out into the warm sunshine.

Nancy shrugged. "It's all right with me."

"I'll make a couple of calls while you order," her father said. "I'll try what you had yesterday—it looked good."

Nancy laughed without humor. "I doubt that either one of us will taste it, but I suppose we have to eat."

Her father patted her shoulder fondly. "We'll find them, honey," he assured her.

While she waited at the table, Nancy tried to find a logical pattern in everything that had happened. But she'd made little sense of it by the time her father sank into the other chair at the table.

"Well?" she asked.

"No calls yet from Nassau," her father answered, "but I did talk to a man about renting a seaplane to take us to Anchor Island."

"When?" Nancy asked.

"The earlier the better," her father replied. "He says landing there after dark is possible, but he'd prefer to get us there in daylight."

"And if no one's there?"

"We'll cross that bridge when we come to it," her father answered. "Right now let's eat our lunch and get back to the hotel to pack. I still have to call Avery before we check out."

Nancy picked up her fork obediently, but tasted little of the food.

Once back at the hotel, Nancy began packing for them both while her father once again placed a call to the authorities in Nassau. This time the discussion was a long one, and after he hung up, he was frowning.

"Did they find them?" Nancy asked.

"No, they don't know where they are, but I spoke to one of the flight attendants who met the girls during their flight to Nassau."

"Did she know what happened to them?" Nancy asked.

"Well, according to her, after the girls passed through customs, they were met by a man who was to take them to Anchor Island."

"What?" Nancy gasped. "But . . ."

"She couldn't give a very good description of the man, just said he was young and was wearing the kind of clothes that a man from a boat would wear: deck shoes, that sort of thing."

"But if the resort is closed, where could he have taken them?" Nancy asked.

Her father could only shake his head. "That is the first question we'll ask the caretaker on Anchor Island."

"When do we leave?"

"As soon as you're ready. I'll call the seaplane port."

7

Anchor Island

The phone rang just as Nancy was closing her suitcase. She hurried out, hoping that it might be further news about Bess and George, but her father shook his head to her inquiring glance.

"That's great, Avery," he was saying. "We'll be by to pick it up on our way to the seaplane." He hung up the phone almost at once. "He has the medallion ready for us."

"Do we have time to pick it up?" Nancy asked, more concerned about getting to Anchor Island than anything else.

"We'll make time. The medallion might have some meaning later on," her father counseled.

Nancy nodded, aware that he was right, but too worried about her friends to find anything else important. She checked the hotel room quickly, then joined her father with her luggage.

"Ready?" he asked.

She nodded.

The drive to Avery Yates's modest seaside home wasn't a long one, and Nancy found the brief visit charming. Happily she agreed that they would spend an entire day with him on their return. His rooms were filled with antique jewelry.

There were photographs of some of the more exotic and valuable collections he'd worked on, but even more interesting were the pieces he displayed himself.

"I'm sorry that I wasn't able to do a complete job on this," Mr. Yates said as he offered the neatly displayed medallion to Nancy.

The box was of polished wood and the medallion glowed richly on a bed of black velvet. "It looks fantastic," she gasped.

"Well, as you can see, this side of the medallion appears to be an anchor's hook. But the other side must have been damaged. I just couldn't raise the second half of the anchor beyond that small jutting point there."

"Do you suppose the artist left the piece unfinished?" Nancy asked.

Mr. Yates considered the idea. "I guess it's possible, but there seems to be some kind of design in that area, so he must have finished something at least."

Nancy touched the glowing metal with her nail, tracing the clearly worked part of the anchor. "A broken anchor," she murmured. "Maybe that's what the artist had in mind!"

"That's as good a guess as any," Mr. Yates answered. "I'll try to find out more about it while you're gone. There are some writings on treasures that were lost in this area of the world. It could be that this is unusual enough to have been mentioned by some old cargo lister."

"That's a subject I'd like to look into," Nancy told him. "Perhaps when we've found Bess and George . . ."

"You're welcome to come anytime, Miss Nancy," he assured her. "I've a small library you could look through."

"We'll call you as soon as we get back," Carson Drew assured him. "And we are grateful for the lovely job you did on this piece."

"I only hope it helps you find your young friends," the old jeweler told them.

The seaplanes were moored to a rough dock, and Nancy had an uneasy feeling as she followed her father to the plane he'd chartered.

The pilot was an unfriendly-appearing man who put their luggage aboard without a smile.

"I don't like starting out this late in the day," he said coldly.

"I'm sorry," Mr. Drew replied. "We've been delayed several times. I was told, however, that a night landing is possible at Anchor Island."

"If we leave now, we'll get there before dark," was the man's only answer.

Carson winked at Nancy, then helped her aboard. To their surprise, they found two men already seated in the cabin.

"I didn't realize there were other passengers," Carson said. "I hope we haven't delayed your trip."

The men smiled politely. "We're going to Swallow Cay," the elder of the two said. "Old Jim said we might ride along, as it's just a short hop from Anchor Island. I hope you don't mind."

"Of course not," Mr. Drew said, then introduced himself and Nancy. The two men introduced themselves as Mr. Perkins and Mr. Graves.

Once they were airborne, Nancy smiled at Mr. Perkins, who was the one across the aisle from her. "Do you know Anchor Island?" she asked.

"I've fished the area," he answered. "Haven't been ashore, though."

"Do you know the DeFoes?" Mr. Drew asked.

"Jeff and Lena, sure," Mr. Graves answered. "Been fishing on the *Polka Dot* with them several times. Are you going to see them?"

"We have friends we think are staying at the Sweet Springs Resort," Mr. Drew answered carefully, his tone telling Nancy that he didn't want to discuss all that had happened with these two strangers.

"Gee, I'd think the place would be closed this time of year," Mr. Perkins said. "Season is pretty well over except for diehard fishermen like us."

"Is the *Polka Dot* the DeFoes' boat?" Nancy asked, intrigued by the name.

"Yes, and it's a nice little cruiser," Mr. Perkins answered. "Two cabins, a good-sized room on the main deck, galley, two modern fishing chairs for working the big game fish—anything you could want. And Lena is a darn good shipboard cook, too." Mr. Perkins grinned. "Better than Ben, anyway."

"You'll be cooking for yourself if you keep that up," Mr. Graves told him.

The two continued to taunt each other and to tell fish stories for the duration of the flight. Nancy listened at first, but then her thoughts went to Bess and George.

She was so deep in her concentration on the mystery of their disappearance that at first she didn't notice the change in the flight. It was Mr. Perkins who brought her attention back to the present.

"There's the island," he said. "You can see the cove where we'll land. It's a great anchorage, probably where they got the name of the island. When the worst hurricanes come, that cove is full of fishing boats."

Nancy leaned forward to peer out the dirty, scarred window as the plane circled over the long, narrow island and dropped lower to enter the cove, which was protected by a long, curving arm of land shaped somewhat like a hook. The beach, which she recognized from the brochure, was deserted, and her heart dropped as she looked up at the abandoned-looking resort, which was built on the spiny highland of the island.

"It does look closed," Carson Drew admitted as the plane settled gracefully to the aqua and green waters of the cove and taxied toward the smooth white length of the concrete dock that extended out into the water.

The plane bumped to a stop and the copilot, who seemed to have the same morose attitude as the pilot, came back to the cabin. "Anchor Island," he announced, moving to open the door.

Nancy unfastened her seat belt and followed him, smelling the sweet flower scents that came on the light breeze that wafted through the door. "We're not sure . . ." she began, wondering what they should do now that they were here. Then a flash of movement on the hill caught her attention.

"I'll get your luggage," the copilot told her, jumping nimbly to the dock and securing the plane with a light rope, then offering her his hand.

"Just a moment, sir," Mr. Drew began. "We don't know yet . . ."

Nancy ran along the dock, not waiting to hear any more. She was halfway to the pale sand of the beach when the figure coming down from the resort appeared between two wildly flowering pin hibiscus plants.

"George!" Nancy shouted, waving frantically. "Oh, George, is it really you?"

"Nancy!" The voice was as unmistakable as the slender, dark-haired form.

Nancy stopped at the end of the dock, waiting as George came running through the last of the plants and out across the sand to meet her. For a moment she just hugged the girl, and then she stepped back to look at her.

"We've been worried sick about you," she told her. "Why didn't you call and tell us that you were here?"

"Oh, Nancy, you . . ." George didn't finish, as the purring of the seaplane suddenly turned to a roar. Both girls turned to watch as the clumsy-looking craft drew away from the dock and made its way out into the cove again, picking up speed till it lifted off the water.

"Nancy, I—" George began, but Nancy lifted a hand.

"Don't say anything till Dad's here," she told her. "He's been worried half to death, too."

Mr. Drew came hurrying along the dock with the luggage. "Where are the resort staff, George?" he asked, setting the suitcases down and mopping his brow in the humid heat of early evening.

"That's what I was about to tell Nancy,"

George answered. "I think we should have kept the seaplane here."

"We can radio Swallow Cay and have them come back for us," Carson Drew said. "I made sure of that before they took off."

George sighed. "I don't know," she said. "We haven't had much luck with the radio so far. Maybe you can make it work."

"Where is everyone?" Nancy asked.

"There's just Penny. The resort is closed, Nancy. Penny was the only one here when we arrived yesterday. She's very nice and we—"

"What do you mean when you arrived yesterday?" Nancy interrupted. "We talked to someone here this morning who said that no one was at the resort, that it was closed."

"You talked to someone on the radio-phone?" George looked skeptical.

"We'd been calling ever since yesterday," Nancy told her.

"Well, you weren't talking to Sweet Springs," George informed them. "The phones haven't worked since we arrived. Otherwise we would have called you last night."

"But . . ." Nancy began, then frowned. "Where is Bess?" she asked.

George looked around. "I don't know," she admitted. "She said she was going for a little walk while Penny and I were working on the radio, but that was an hour ago."

"Maybe she's taking a nap," Nancy suggested. "Though she should have heard the plane."

George shook her head. "I was in our room when I heard it. She must be with Penny."

A pert redhead appeared on the beach at that moment, a ready smile of welcome lighting her green eyes. "You must be the Drews," she said. "George and Bess have told me so much about you. I'm Penny DeFoe."

For a moment they were busy with introductions and greetings, Nancy and her father surprised and excited at hearing the name DeFoe. But before they could ask the girl about her name, George asked, "Penny, have you seen Bess?"

Penny frowned. "I thought she was with you," she answered.

There was a moment of silence, and then they all looked at each other, suddenly aware of the empty beach and the deepening shadows. Where was Bess?

8

Search for Bess

"Let's get your things up to the resort," Penny said. "Then we can organize a search for Bess. She can't have wandered far, and since we're alone on the island, she's not in any danger."

"Alone on the island?" Mr. Drew gasped. "But surely there's someone?"

Penny shook her curly head. "I was really lonesome till Bess and George arrived."

"What about the DeFoes?" Nancy asked. "Jeff and Lena: are they your parents?"

"Grandparents," the twenty-year-old answered. "And I honestly don't know where they are. I arrived just the day before yesterday and there was a note waiting for me, saying that

I should make myself at home, that I'd be hearing from them soon. Nothing more."

Nancy looked from the redhead to George.

"Do they do that often?" Carson Drew asked Penny.

"They've never done anything like that before," Penny answered. Nancy could see the worry in her open face. "They invited me to spend the summer with them, and the last time I talked to them, they were just full of plans for things we'd be doing." She sighed. "I was a little surprised when they didn't meet me in Nassau, but I took the island ferry over."

"What about you, George?" Nancy asked. "How did you and Bess get here?"

"A man called Tom came up to us at the airport. He asked Bess if she was Nancy Drew, and she said that she wasn't, but that we were here to take your place. He seemed a little unhappy about it, but he told us he'd been sent from Sweet Springs to pick us up." She shrugged. "He brought us as far as the dock in his boat, unloaded our suitcases, and just left."

Penny grinned. "I was so glad to see them. I didn't know what arrangements my grandparents had made, but I'd missed having someone to talk to." She paused as they reached the resort building. "Welcome to Sweet Springs Resort," she said.

"Bess," George shouted. "Bess, where are you? Nancy and Mr. Drew are here."

Her words echoed hollowly through the large, comfortable reception area and into the dimness beyond. There was no answer except the soft whispering of the palm fronds above them and the sighing of the waves as they lapped against the well-protected beach.

"I hope you don't mind taking the rooms next to the one Bess and George have been sharing," Penny continued. "The cabins are nicer, but I haven't had time to make them up, and the staff had closed them and covered everything before they left the island."

"Is that usual?" Carson Drew asked after assuring her that any room would be fine. "I mean that everyone left the island that way."

"Pretty much," Penny answered. "Most of the people who work in the resort live on the nearby islands, so they go home as soon as my grandparents close for the summer."

The rooms were small, but handsomely appointed and quite comfortable. Nancy was pleased to see that all three rooms were linked by a narrow, roofed balcony that was reached by sliding glass doors in each room. Still, her pleasure was tempered by the fact that there was no sign of Bess anywhere.

As soon as the luggage was placed in the room, Carson Drew turned to Penny. "George mentioned a radio-phone," he said. "Do you think I might use it? I'd like to try to contact the seaplane and ask for some kind of help."

"I'll be happy to let you use it," Penny answered. "Maybe it will work for you. George and I haven't been able to get anything on it so far."

"Someone called us from here," Nancy told the redhead. "At least, we were calling this resort, so I assumed the man I talked to was here. He said that the resort was closed and he was alone on the island. He claimed he was the caretaker."

Penny frowned. "That's not possible, Nancy."

"The call must have come from another island," George said.

Nancy started to protest that the man had mentioned the name of the resort, then let it go with a shrug. "While Dad is trying to get help,

68

why don't we go look for Bess?" she suggested. "Maybe she sprained an ankle or something."

George nodded. "She's not going to want to be out there alone after dark."

Nancy noticed that the light was indeed beginning to dim, and she was well aware of the shortness of the twilight in the area. "Where could she have gone?" she asked George and Penny.

"Beats me," George said. "She spent most of today lying on the beach and walking around the edge of the cove."

Nancy sighed, looking around at the thick growth of tropical plants and flowers. Had everything been less orderly, it would have resembled a jungle.

"I doubt that Bess would have gone far from the resort," George said, echoing Nancy's thoughts perfectly.

Nancy smiled at her. "She's not that adventurous," she agreed.

Penny led the way outside. "Why don't you two take the beach," she suggested. "I'll explore around the cabins and in the gardens, since I know them better."

"Good thinking," Nancy agreed, starting toward the path that led to the beach. "We can meet back here as soon as we finish. Maybe by then Dad will have made some contact with the radio-phone."

"I hope so," Penny said. But her tone didn't hold a great deal of confidence.

Nancy followed George to the beach, which was not very wide. They stopped and looked in both directions.

"I guess we won't be able to find any footprints in the sand," George observed, watching as the waves lapped the damp sand, erasing all marks. "The dry sand won't hold prints and the waves take any in the wet sand."

"Well, we could see her anyway if she was on the sand," Nancy reminded her. "But if we follow the inside edge of the beach, we should be able to see her footprints leading off the beach."

"You're right," George complimented her. "Let's get started while we still have some light. This place really gets spooky at night."

"You think so?" Nancy was surprised at the comment from the usually down-to-earth George.

"It's because there's no one else on the island," George explained. "No lights, no noise except for the waves, wind, birds, and cats that roam wild on the island. The chickens run wild, too, but they're quiet at night."

"It does sound eerie," Nancy admitted. "So let's find Bess before it gets dark."

The two girls followed the line of flowering plants that formed the edge of the beach. Nancy quickly slipped off her shoes, enjoying the feeling of the warm sand on her bare feet as she peered into the shadowy area behind the plants. The ground there was still sandy, but much firmer than the beach. There were marks in it, but nothing that resembled a footprint.

The arm of land curved and grew narrower, so that sometimes she could catch small glimpses of the rocks that formed the outer edge of the land and could hear the more violent crashing of the waves on them. Palms shaded the area and the plants.

Nancy was almost to the end of the sand when something caught her eye. There was a tiny flash of bright blue among the soft greens of the remaining plants that clung to the narrowing ridge of land.

Nancy paused, then moved into the shade of

the palm fronds and picked up a small triangle of cloth. She recognized it as coming from a flared skirt that she knew was one of Bess's favorites. She saw the footprints immediately.

"George," she called to her friend, who had fallen behind to examine a shell. "I think I've found something over here."

"Nancy, did you find Bess?" It was her father calling down the hill from the resort.

"Just footprints," Nancy shouted.

"We'll be right down," Carson called.

Nancy and George waited, watching as Penny and Nancy's father came down the path from the resort. Neither of them was smiling.

"Any luck with the radio-phone, Dad?" Nancy asked as they neared them.

He shook his head. "There's something wrong, but I didn't take the time to really look for the trouble. Perhaps this evening. Now, what did you find?"

"This." Nancy extended the scrap of material. "Bess's skirt?" she asked George.

George nodded. "She was wearing it today."

"The footprints lead this way," Nancy continued, stepping past the barrier of plants and following the marks through the shadowy area and coming out on the other side. There she stopped, her rising hopes dropping abruptly.

"Where do they go?" Penny asked from behind her.

"Nowhere," Nancy answered, her voice close to a wail. "They stop right here!" She pointed to the rocks that stood against the onslaught of the waves crashing against the shore.

9

Phantom Intruders

The footprints did indeed stop at the rocks. Nancy looked at them carefully. "She must have walked on the rocks," she murmured, stepping up on the nearest boulder and standing on it to look around.

"But where did she go from here?" George asked.

Nancy shook her head. "I have no idea," she admitted.

"Maybe we should just go back along the rocks toward the resort," her father suggested. "She couldn't have gone the other direction, could she?"

They all followed his gaze. The rocky shore

extended a hundred yards, curving around to the entrance of the cove. The trees and brush ended nearby, and there was a clear view of the protective rocks.

"I'll walk on the rocks," Nancy said, "and the rest of you watch for footprints." The plants on this side of the arm of land were much less lush, and she was sure that Bess would be plainly visible if she'd left the rocks.

Nancy moved toward the resort, hopping as easily from rock to rock as she assumed Bess had. At first it was simple enough, since the rocks were close together and fairly smooth on top. Then however, the coastline grew rougher. Nancy made a long jump from one rock to another, and her foot slipped.

"Careful, honey," her father said, catching her arm as she stumbled to the sand.

"Bess would never have been able to make that jump," George commented firmly.

"There'd be no reason for her to," Nancy agreed. "I was trying to stay out of the sand just to see if I could."

"But where could she have gone?" Penny asked, looking back the way they'd come. "We didn't find any more tracks, Nancy."

Nancy followed her gaze, trying to find

another explanation or another way that Bess could have gone, but there was nothing. Areas of crusted sand separated the rocky outcroppings and there were no tracks to mar them.

"Would she have gone into the water?" Carson Drew asked, his gaze directed to George.

George shook her head without hesitation. "Penny warned us about the tides on this side of the island," she replied. "We swam only in the cove where it's safe. Besides, Bess wouldn't be swimming in her clothes—her bathing suit is still hanging on the balcony rail drying out."

After several more minutes of looking around the area, they all followed Penny through the screening growth of hibiscus and other plants and back along the beach to the path that led up to the resort. There Nancy paused.

"Isn't there somewhere else we could look?" she asked.

Penny sighed. "Not around the cove," she replied. "We can search the resort area and look in the cabins again and along the paths to them, but that's really about all there is on this end of the island—and I did just search them."

"What's on the other end?" Carson Drew asked.

"Well, there's a small road that leads along

the ridge, and at the far end of it is a little village. The regular dock is there. That's where the inter-island ferry stops when it has a passenger for Anchor Island."

"When will it be stopping again?" Nancy asked quickly.

Penny shrugged. "The next time someone wants to come here, or if they have a delivery for us. In the winter, they come three times a week; but in the off-season, they might not come for weeks."

Nancy looked at her father, reading the same worry in his face that she was feeling.

"Are you sure there is no one else on the island, Penny?" Mr. Drew asked.

The redhead considered for a moment, then shrugged. "We haven't seen anyone, Mr. Drew. And there's really no reason why anyone would be here. The village is just the houses the staff stay in during the winter, and there's no one at the resort but us, of that I am sure."

George nodded. "We explored this end of the island today," she said, "and we didn't see anything or anyone but Penny."

"Well, then I guess we'd better go back to the resort," Nancy conceded with a sigh. "Maybe Bess is waiting there."

The rest smiled at her words, but she sensed that they had no more confidence in that than she did. Bess wouldn't have waited quietly for them to return. If she had come to the resort and found it empty, she would have been looking for them just as they were looking for her.

"You didn't find anything in the resort grounds, did you?" George asked Penny.

The older girl shook her head. "No footprints, nothing. I checked the cabins, too, and they're all still locked up."

"Then where can she be?" George asked.

"Could we check the other end of the island?" Mr. Drew asked.

"Not till morning," Penny answered.

"Why not?" Nancy inquired, startled by her words. "If Bess is there—"

"We can go," Penny amended quickly, "but there's no electricity going to that end of the island now, so I don't know how much searching we could do."

"What do you mean there's no electricity?" Mr. Drew asked.

"The two ends of the island are served by separate generators," Penny answered. "Luckily, my grandparents left the generator on here. I have no idea how to turn them on."

"Dad, do you think you. . ." Nancy began.

Her father chuckled. "I could try, but I doubt that I could manage it in the dark. Besides," his grin deepened. "I can't imagine that Bess would have taken such a hike. This island must be close to a mile and a half long."

Nancy had to nod, knowing that he was right about Bess. Long hikes were not her favorite exercise. Her smile faded, however, as they reached the top of the path and she looked up at the main resort building.

Darkness was coming quickly now, and the lovely building no longer looked warm and welcoming as it had earlier. No light burned inside and the silence seemed threatening.

"I guess I'd better get to the kitchen and start dinner," Penny began, looking guilty. "I'm afraid I'm not much of a cook, but. . ."

"We'll come with you," Nancy assured her. "Whatever is going on here, it's obvious that we really aren't supposed to be guests here."

"Oh, but if my grandparents invited you. . ." Penny said, looking uncomfortable. "Where are they, Mr. Drew? Nancy?" she asked.

Nancy looked at her father, not sure how to answer the question.

He sighed. "I'm sure George and Bess told you about the contest prize letter that Nancy received," he began.

Penny nodded.

"Well, the reason that Nancy and I didn't come here immediately was because we were asked to look at an abandoned boat in Florida, a boat that we now believe belongs to your grandparents."

"The *Polka Dot*?" Penny looked shocked. "But they would never have abandoned it, Mr. Drew. And why would they be in Florida?"

"I really don't know the answers to any of that," he admitted. "We were called in because there was a folder of clippings about Nancy found on board. All other identification of the boat was removed."

"Then how did you know that it belongs to my grandparents?" Penny asked.

"We aren't positive," Nancy admitted. "The sheriff made the identification, but—"

"Couldn't Penny identify the boat for him?" George asked. "I mean after we get off here."

"She probably can," Nancy agreed. "Only the boat disappeared some time last night. The sheriff blamed us at first. He didn't even want to let us come here to look for you and Bess."

The mention of Bess stopped the conversation for a moment, then Penny spoke. "But where are my grandparents?" she asked. "They must be somewhere."

"I'll tell you everything we know," Carson Drew said, a fatherly arm resting on her shoulders as he led her to one of the couches.

"We'll go start dinner," George said, drawing Nancy away.

The lights they turned on as they passed from the lobby area through the handsome dining room and on into the spacious kitchen helped lift a little of the gloom, but Nancy was still conscious of Bess's absence. "What do we have to work with?" she asked, looking around the room.

"Most anything you want," George answered. "There's a big freezer full of meat and fish, and there's loads of canned stuff. Fresh fruit and vegetables are about all that we don't have. Penny says they have to come in by boat. What do you think is going on?" she asked.

Nancy shrugged. "Well, if the boat is the *Polka Dot*, I'd say that the contest prize was definitely meant to get Dad and me to come down here. Someone read about us in the papers and thought it was the perfect way to attract our attention."

George grinned. "And got us instead."

"I think it's more than that," Nancy continued. "I mean, if it was the DeFoes, why would they go to Florida if they were expecting us and Penny, too."

George nodded. "You're right about that. And that note that Penny found. She says it's her grandmother's handwriting all right, but the message seems strange. What kind of a note is that to leave for someone you've invited to spend the summer?"

"Could I see it?" Nancy asked, aware that she was grasping at straws.

"As soon as we get something started for dinner, we can ask Penny where it is." George moved to the huge old freezer with confidence. "Now, do you want to cook something or shall we just heat one of the casseroles?"

"Casseroles?" Nancy asked, arching an eyebrow.

"The freezer is full of them, and they're good, too. Penny says that the resort chef fixes them from the leftovers every day during the season.

They eat some of them and so does the staff, but the rest they freeze for the summer."

"That sounds fine to me," Nancy said. "I'm so worried about Bess, I'm not really hungry."

"I just don't know what could have happened to her," George admitted. "It was just kind of hot in the office where Penny and I were working, so Bess said she'd go out and take a little walk to cool off." She looked miserable. "I guess I should have gone with her."

"Oh, George, don't blame yourself," Nancy responded quickly while she helped her take things out of the freezer. "You certainly couldn't know that she was going to disappear."

"But I should—" George began, then stopped as a scream came from outside the well-lit kitchen. "Penny?" she shouted.

Nancy ran through the door into the dining room, then followed the sounds across to the lobby and into the small room behind the big resort desk. There she found both Penny and her father.

"What in the world. . ." Nancy asked, then stopped as she followed their horrified gaze to the sturdy table in the corner. "What was that?" she gasped.

"The radio-phone," her father answered, his

eyes leaving the wreckage to meet her gaze.

"But what. . . ?" George began. "Who wrecked the radio-phone?"

"It would seem," Carson Drew said, "that we are not alone on this island."

10

The Pirate Legend

"But," Penny began. "Who would do something like that?"

"Someone who doesn't want us to reach anyone outside the island," Nancy answered promptly. "Right, Dad?"

Her father nodded, his face grim. "What worries me is why they don't want us to make calls."

"I'd like to get my hands on whoever did this," Penny said. "That radio-phone cost my grandparents a lot of money and they need it to run this resort."

"I'm sure we'll find out who and why," George murmured.

Watching a look of helplessness grow in Nancy's eyes, Mr. Drew touched her cheek lightly. "We're all worried about Bess, Nancy," he told her. "But there's nothing we can do in the dark—especially now that we know there's someone out there."

"What should I do?" Penny asked.

"I think it might be a good idea to lock up," Nancy said. "I realize it's too late for us to protect this." She waved a hand at the destroyed radio-phone. "But I would like to know that we're safe here tonight."

"But if they're already inside the building," Penny protested.

"We'll lock the doors, then search the whole building," Carson Drew explained.

"How do you suppose anyone knew that we were here to use the radio-phone?" Nancy asked.

"Tom!" George gasped. "We thought the DeFoes had sent him, but now I wonder. They would have had him meet Penny, too, wouldn't they?"

Nancy nodded. "But he must have known about the tickets," she reminded her. "He was looking for me at the airport. But you didn't know we were coming, did you, Penny?"

The girl shook her curls. "If they told him to

meet you, maybe he knows where they are. I really want to know what's going on."

"So do we," Mr. Drew assured her. "Now, if you'll show me what should be locked up, Penny, we can secure the resort."

"While we see to dinner," Nancy agreed.

"Good girl," her father murmured, giving the radio-phone one last glance, then shaking his head.

"What could anyone want around here?" George asked Nancy as they resumed their interrupted dinner preparations.

Nancy shook her head. "You've seen more of the place than I have."

"It's beautiful, but there's nothing to steal. I mean, it's the resort itself that's valuable. It just doesn't make sense, Nancy. Nothing does."

Nancy had to agree. "Nothing has made sense since I got the tickets."

The search of the resort building didn't take long, and by the time they returned to the kitchen, the casserole was beginning to fill the air with a delicious scent. George sniffed appreciatively. "If Bess is nearby, that will get her back here in a hurry," she joked, though her eyes told Nancy that she was far from lighthearted.

"Do you think that whoever is on the island is

holding her prisoner?" Nancy asked, putting into words the fear that had been haunting her since she'd seen the vandalized radio-phone.

"Why would they take Bess?" Penny asked.

"Perhaps she saw them," Carson Drew suggested. "You did say that she went out for a walk alone."

"But why would they care?" Nancy asked.

There was no answer to that question, so they continued setting the table in silence. Penny sighed as she surveyed the food that Nancy and George had produced from the kitchen.

"I'm sorry I can't offer any fresh fruits or vegetables," she said. "My grandparents have a standing order with the ferry to bring in fresh goods every week, but I've checked the dock and nothing has been delivered so far."

"Perhaps they left word to stop the deliveries while they were gone," George suggested.

"But why would they leave if they knew that Penny was arriving?" Nancy asked. "That really doesn't make sense."

"Do you think whoever is on the island is staying in the village?" George asked, changing the subject slightly.

"I suppose they could be," Penny admitted.

Nancy said nothing for a moment, her mind

busy; then she smiled a little. "If they came to the island by boat, maybe we could find out where it's docked," she suggested. "That way, one of us could go for help."

"Or radio," Penny said. "Most boats in this area have radios on board."

"I hope we find it fast," George said.

Nancy nodded her agreement, then turned to Penny. "Do you have any idea why your grandparents would want my father and me here?" she asked. "Have they ever mentioned a mystery about the resort or the island?"

Penny considered for a moment, then shook her head. "I can't remember anything. Of course, I haven't spent much time here the last few years, but before that I did lots of exploring on the island. It had no secrets then."

"I suppose it could have been someone else who sent the tickets," Carson Drew admitted.

"But why would someone else want us here?" Nancy asked.

"Perhaps it has something to do with the medallion," her father suggested.

"What medallion?" Penny and George asked.

Nancy gasped, realizing that in her worry over Bess's disappearance she hadn't even thought about the beautiful golden antique necklace. She jumped to her feet and ran to her room, suddenly afraid that it, too, might have disappeared.

Surprisingly, the black box was still in her purse when she opened it and she took a moment to look at the lovely medallion before carrying it out to the dining room. There she handed it to Penny. "Do you know anything about this?" she asked.

Penny's eyes grew round in astonishment.

"What is it?" George asked. "What does it mean?" She, too, stared at the beautiful piece of golden workmanship.

"I never believed that it existed," Penny gasped. "I mean Grandpa told me stories about it all the time when I was little, but I always thought ... He told me that it was just a legend." She looked across the table at Nancy. "Where did you get this?"

Nancy explained quickly about losing her earring and finding the necklace beneath the floorboards. As she spoke, Penny's face paled and the excitement of seeing the necklace faded back into worry and fear.

"What is it, Penny?" Carson Drew asked as Nancy finished her description.

"The abandoned boat was the *Polka Dot*,"

Penny gasped. "Where Nancy found this proves it. The place you found the necklace Grandpa calls his 'hidey hole.' He always kept any money he had on the boat in there or any valuables they were carrying. Said it was safer there than in his wallet or in Grandma's purse."

"Then you think your grandparents put the medallion in there?" Nancy asked.

Penny nodded. "But where would they get something like this?"

"What do you know about the necklace?" Nancy asked, unable to answer Penny's question.

"Well, the legend says that it belonged to some pirate, that he wore it at all times and guarded it with his life. He was an island man who hated and feared the Spaniards and raided their galleons whenever he had the chance." Penny paused to take a sip of her iced tea.

"So did he succeed as a pirate?" George asked impatiently.

"According to legend, there were three Spanish ships sailing in the area that were separated when a terrible storm hit. Two of the ships managed to stay afloat till the storm cleared and they found their way back to each other. But the third was nowhere to be seen."

Penny paused as though expecting comment, but no one spoke, so she went on. "The two ships searched and searched till they came upon a tiny island with wreckage on the beach. The Spanish sailors rowed to shore and discovered that it was from the galleon. They searched some more and found a few survivors, but no one who could tell them what had happened." Penny stopped again, her eyes sparkling.

"What do you mean what had happened?" Nancy asked, her imagination caught by the story. "Didn't the ship break up on the island?"

Penny shook her auburn curls. "The wreckage was a small boat from the galleon and they soon learned that all the survivors had been in that boat and that they'd left the galleon without knowing for sure that it was going to sink." Penny smiled.

"You mean that people thought the pirate had taken the galleon?" Mr. Drew asked.

Penny nodded. "The necklace was supposed to be part of the bounty he took from the galleon—the only part of it that was ever seen by anyone else."

"You mean that's the legend?" Nancy was both intrigued and a little disappointed.

"That's one of them. I've heard all sorts of stories. That's why I never really believed there was a necklace. And this might not be the one from the legend. I mean, I'm sure there are lots of antique gold necklaces from that era, so . . ." Her smile faded.

"That's what the man who restored it for us said," Nancy admitted.

"Only I think my grandparents would probably know about it—if it was genuine or not, I mean. Grandpa was always reading about the legend and talking to old-timers around here. That's where he got so many stories to tell me."

Nancy reached out a hand to take the medallion from the girl. She studied it carefully, wishing that Mr. Yates had been able to bring out the entire design instead of just the strange hook.

"Do you think this could be why your grandparents sent me the tickets?" she asked at last. "I mean, if they really thought this was the necklace in the legend."

"I'd be willing to bet on it," Penny answered. She stopped with a gasp as the lights suddenly went out—leaving them in almost absolute blackness.

11

Blackout

"What happened?" Nancy gasped, her fingers automatically closing around the medallion box.

"Someone has cut the electricity, I imagine," Mr. Drew answered quietly. "Where is the generator, Penny?"

"It's back along the ridge. There's a small building that protects it, and the wires carry the electricity to the cabins and to the main building from there."

"Then it would be very easy for someone to cut power to the resort," Nancy murmured.

"Just sit still," Penny ordered. "I know where there are candles and hurricane lamps. My grandmother keeps matches and everything we need handy because of the storms that pass through here and blow down the lines."

They waited, hearing the sound of her chair, the whisper of her soft shoes on the tiled floor, the small noises of her passage through the forest of tables and chairs that blocked the area, and then the unmistakable opening of a drawer. A match flared and a candle caught.

At first the light seemed too feeble, but then as their eyes adjusted the shadows appeared to recede. More candles were lit, then four hurricane lamps bloomed to life.

"That's better," Penny murmured, her hand shaking only a little as she carried one lamp back to the table, leaving the others on the old-fashioned sideboard.

"Does that generator power anything else?" Carson Drew asked.

Penny looked confused for a moment. "Just the electrical appliances. The water comes from the spring that gave the resort its name, and the water heater and cooking facilities are gas."

"So we basically have a blackout," George summed it up.

"That's about it," Penny agreed.

Nancy, however, was staring beyond them to the dark world outside the windows that gave a panoramic view of the cove and the ocean beyond. Suddenly she shivered—not from the cold, for the night was warm, but because she felt eyes in that darkness.

"What is it, Nancy?" her father asked gently.

"They must be out there," Nancy answered. "Watching us, listening to what we say."

"And seeing the necklace," George gasped, moving to drop her napkin over the gleaming medallion.

"Could that be what they're after?" Carson Drew asked Penny while he moved to drop the bamboo shade that had been rolled up above the window.

Penny hurried to help him cover all the windows. "I don't know," she admitted. "If they knew about it, it would certainly be valuable enough for someone to want to steal."

"But it wasn't here," Nancy reminded them both. "We found it in Florida."

"On the *Polka Dot*." Her father's tone was thoughtful.

They sat in cozy silence, the world shut out by the shades, the flickering lamplight giving the large room a rather intimate air. Nancy stared at the half-hidden medallion, remembering only too well the way she'd showed it around to George and Penny—and to whomever might have been watching outside.

"Do you have a safe or something where the medallion could be kept?" Carson Drew asked.

"There's an office safe," Penny answered. "But I don't know the combination, and anyway, I can open it with a bent hairpin."

"That doesn't sound too safe," George told her.

"Living on an island, people don't do too much about security," Penny admitted. "There's no easy place to run if you steal something, so most people just don't bother."

"Your grandfather doesn't have a 'hidey hole' in the resort, does he?" Nancy asked.

Penny shrugged. "If he does, he didn't tell me where it is," she replied.

Nancy sighed. "I'm beginning to wish we'd left this with Sheriff Boyd," she said.

"We'll just have to find a place to hide it here," her father told her.

"What about putting it on ice?" George suggested softly.

"What?" Penny looked at the brunette as though she thought she'd lost her senses.

"With the rest of the leftovers?" Nancy asked, her blue eyes brightening.

"We'd better cover the windows in the

kitchen first," her father reminded them.

"Good idea," Nancy said. "I feel as if there's someone watching me all the time now."

"I'll pull down the shades while you two get the cake and ice cream for dessert," Penny told Nancy and George.

Carson agreed. "Bring back a dish and some plastic wrap for the necklace. We want it to blend right in with the rest of the frozen food."

Nancy giggled, feeling better. At least they were fighting back against their unseen adversaries. "So let's do it," she said.

It went surprisingly well. The necklace was carefully enclosed in plastic wrap, then after a bit of discussion, placed in the middle of a loaf of frozen bread.

"If we put it in a new package, they might look for it," Nancy explained. "But who would think to go through a whole stack of frozen loaves of bread?"

"Sheer genius," Penny told her. "Now if you could just figure out how to get the electricity fixed before things start to thaw . . ."

"How long do we have?" Nancy asked.

"Probably a couple of days if we don't open the freezer much," Penny answered. "A large freezer like this full of frozen food can hold up quite a while. Of course, the dishwasher is another matter."

Nancy laughed. "I guess we'll just have to do dishes the old-fashioned way," she said. "After that, maybe we could look at the note your grandmother left and anything else that might give us a clue to what happened to them."

"And to Bess," George murmured sadly.

Nancy's light-heartedness faded immediately.

"I'm afraid we have to face the fact that they have her," she admitted.

"But where?" George asked.

"That's what we're going to try to find out tomorrow," Nancy replied, trying her best to sound more confident than she felt.

"It's going to be a long night," George prophesied.

Though Nancy had agreed with her friend, they were both wrong. Exhausted by all that had happened and lulled by the soft sounds of the night wind, Nancy slept deeply, waking just as the first rays of the sun entered her room through a tiny chink in the drapes.

Bess! Memories of her missing friend swept away the seeds of sleep and had her on her feet at once. She washed quickly and pulled on a pair of blue shorts and a top. A long look out the window at the scene beyond told her that their intruders were nowhere to be seen in the beautiful morning.

Opening the glass door to the balcony, she stepped outside and sniffed the sweet flower scents that rode the cool morning air. It was a lovely day and she could see the multicolored water in the cove and the gleaming pale sand that edged it. If she hadn't been so worried about Bess, she would have found the island and its mysteries enchanting.

"See anything, Nancy?" George asked.

A rooster crowed off to their right and was immediately answered by a second crow to the left. "What in the world is that all about?" she asked.

"Island alarm clocks, Penny calls them," George answered. "She says they're wild chickens. The descendants of some that were abandoned on the island one spring when everyone left for the summer."

"It looks so peaceful," Nancy mused, frowning at the tranquil scene before them.

"We thought that it was," George told her. "We were really enjoying ourselves."

Nancy sighed, then straightened her shoulders resolutely. "Well, let's go see what there is for breakfast. The sooner we eat, the sooner we can start a search for Bess. She has to be somewhere on this island and we have to find her."

"Right," George agreed as they left the pretty view and went into the dim hallway.

They were just halfway along the corridor when Carson Drew opened his door and joined them. "Did you hear anything during the night?" he asked.

Nancy and George shook their heads. "Did you, Dad?" Nancy inquired.

"Not a sound," he replied. "I guess our security measures must have been enough."

"I suppose we should check the doors, just to be sure," George said. "I'll go make sure the kitchen is still locked."

"I'll get the front," Nancy agreed, hurrying across the lobby area to test the door and finding it firmly locked. She took two steps back toward the dining room, then stopped.

She hurried to roll up the shades that they'd closed the night before, then gasped. The door to the office safe, which Penny had showed them earlier, hung open, and the desk had been thoroughly searched. Someone had been in the resort while they slept!

12

An Unexplained Break-in

"Dad," she called softly, suddenly aware that she might not be alone in the dim room.

"Find something, Nancy?" her father asked, coming to lean on the desk.

She pointed to the safe, not speaking. He looked at it for a moment, then went to check the main door of the office, which was securely locked. Nancy looked in the small lavatory and the closet that opened off the office, then made a more thorough search of the lobby and dining room before going on to the kitchen.

"What took you so long?" George asked. "Penny and I have breakfast almost under control."

"Is everything all right out here?" Nancy

asked, indicating with her glance that she was talking about the necklace in the freezer.

George caught the warning in Nancy's gaze. "Everything is fine, why?"

"The safe is open and the desk has been searched," Nancy answered, her gaze on Penny, hoping that the girl wouldn't give away the hiding place they'd chosen for the golden medallion. "We don't know if the people are still in the building or not," she declared.

"But how could anyone get in?" Penny asked. "The back door was securely locked and so was the front. I checked them this morning."

"Dad is trying to find out now," Nancy answered. "The doors lock with keys, don't they? I mean, you can't just push a button to lock them from the inside."

Penny patted her shorts pocket. "I've got the resort set right here."

"How did you get in when you got here?" George asked.

Penny looked startled for a moment, then shook her head. "I was so upset, I didn't even think about it," she began. "It was unlocked. The keys were hanging on the nail over there." She indicated the small key board which held several other keys with tags saying that they unlocked the generator building and the cabins that were scattered in the trees and bushes.

"You mean your grandparents just went off and left the place unlocked?" Nancy asked.

"Well, at the time I just thought maybe they had gone out fishing. With no one else on the island, locking up doesn't seem too important."

"But if the doors were locked last night and neither one was forced, how did anyone open the safe?" George asked.

"They forced it," Carson Drew answered from the doorway. "As Penny said, it wasn't too difficult, though I'm surprised they were able to do it without waking any of us. They must have had keys. The windows and glass doors are all still locked and there's no sign of anyone having forced the door locks that I can see." He moved to inspect the outside of the kitchen door.

"But how could they have keys?" George asked.

"Who does have keys to this building, Penny?" Nancy asked. "Besides your grandparents, I mean."

Penny shrugged. "I have no idea," she admitted. "I suppose some of the staff have their own keys, but I wouldn't know which ones."

Nancy sighed. "Well, let's get breakfast. Then we can go out and search the village."

"And find Bess," George agreed.

"Is everything else all right?" Carson Drew asked.

"There are plenty of good things in the freezer, Mr. Drew," George answered with a wink. "I checked that first thing."

Mr. Drew nodded. "That's very important since we have no idea how long we'll have to stay here. Now, I'll go see if I can get the electricity hooked up again before everything in there thaws out."

"Does anyone else on the island have a radio that they might have left here?" Nancy asked after her father left. "We really should make some kind of contact with the outside world."

"We can check today," Penny answered, then smiled at them. "I hope everyone likes the blueberry pancakes and ham."

"Sounds heavenly," Nancy replied, "but I do wonder what Bess has been eating."

"Don't we all," George agreed.

The lights came on just as they began dishing out the food, but worry about Bess clouded their enjoyment of the meal and Carson's success with the generator. They hurried through the cleanup, anxious to be on their way to search the village as well as the land between the resort and the small settlement.

"So how do you want to organize this search?" Penny asked when they stepped outside into the warm sunlit morning.

"How much land is there to search?" Nancy asked.

"You can see most of it from the road," Penny replied, pointing to the dirt pathway that led from the rear of the resort building along a palm-lined ridge of land. "That's the highest point of the island. It's like a spine that runs the whole length from the resort on this end to a sort of valley where the village is built."

"Then we could see anyone on either side of the narrow part?" Mr. Drew asked.

"I think so," Penny answered. "I used to hike along the shore on either side, but it's very rocky and hard going."

"Perhaps we should search this area again before we go," Carson Drew suggested, gesturing toward the paths that radiated from the main building. "Someone could be using the keys to stay in the cabins, couldn't they?"

They all agreed, and so began their search with the cabins. They found them charming, each one tucked into its own bower of hibiscus and well shaded by palms and other tropical growth. They were, however, all disappointingly empty, the debris of fallen blossoms and leaves that coated their small porches making it clear that no one had entered or left recently.

Nancy cast a longing glance at the beach and the deserted dock with the two small boats tied to it. She remembered how excited she'd been when they'd arrived in the seaplane and when she had actually seen George coming down to meet them. If only Bess had been with her.

"You walk on one side, and I'll walk on the other, George," Nancy suggested. "That way we can keep a clear eye on the area below. If we can't see behind trees or bushes, we can go down and check them out."

"That sounds like a good plan," Penny agreed. "We'll all watch."

The searching made progress slow, but they were at least confident that they hadn't overlooked anything by the time they reached the final dip in the road that led down to the small village. Nancy stopped on the hill, startled and depressed by what she was seeing.

"I know it isn't really a village," Penny explained, "but I didn't know what else to call it."

The half-dozen houses were all clustered around a small open area where a large fig tree spread its branches, shading several battered benches. Chickens wandered busily through the remains of gardens that had been planted behind some of the houses, and a large calico cat slept on the porch rail of one of the houses.

"It sure looks deserted," George observed.

They started down the hill, Nancy studying the one well-painted and maintained building in the area—the small structure that served what appeared to be a public dock. "Do you have keys to the houses, Penny?" Nancy asked.

"I doubt we'll need them," Penny said. "Most people don't bother to lock up here."

As they reached the small valley, the four of them fanned out, each heading for a different house, eager to find Bess or some sign of the person who'd opened the safe at the resort. Their hopes were quickly dashed, however.

Though the houses varied slightly in size, they were basically the same in layout—two bedrooms in the rear, a large main room across the front, and a screened porch beyond that. The furnishings were old and worn but comfortable-looking, and there were plenty of things left behind to show that the tenants planned to return. All that was missing was any sign at all of recent occupants.

"I don't think Bess was ever here," George said as she stepped out of the final house. "There's just no sign of her or anyone else."

"But if she's not here, where can she be?" Nancy asked, looking around.

"And where is our thief from last night?" Penny asked, frowning just as the others were.

"Is there any place else on the island where they could hide?" Carson Drew asked.

Penny considered, then shook her head. "There's just the resort and the village."

"But where . . ." George began, then stopped as she saw that Nancy's gaze had gone from her to the public dock and the small building situated there.

"I don't think anyone . . ." Penny started to say as she led them up the steps to the concrete slab that formed the inland end of the dock.

Nancy hurried after her, rounding the corner of the building at a trot, then stopped, her heart sinking once again. What had appeared to be a building from the island was little more than a three-sided shed with the open side facing the sea. There were protective doors and shutters, but they stood open to the warm breeze. The interior was a shadowed muddle of boxes and crates, cupboards, and a long flat counter.

"This is sure a mess," George observed as she peered into the interior.

"Always," Penny agreed. "Everybody uses it as extra storage in the summer. In the winter Old Joe runs the dock and he keeps things pretty tidy."

"It doesn't look like Bess or the others were here," Nancy said, wiping off her hand after having rested it on the counter.

"*Someone* was," Penny observed, her tone changing as she moved around the corner and made her way to the pigeonholes in the rear of the shed. She reached up and took a piece of white paper out of one and carried it back out into the sunlight, frowning.

"What is it?" Nancy asked.

"It's a bill from the grocery supplier that my grandparents use," Penny answered. "A list of supplies that were left here yesterday by the

111

inter-island ferry." Penny handed the bill to Nancy and her father. "Supplies that we certainly didn't get."

Nancy scanned the list and felt a chill. "That's enough food to feed a half-dozen people," she gasped.

George looked around nervously. "So where is it?" she asked.

13

Polka Dot *Sighting*

"Are there any nearby islands?" Carson Drew asked Penny.

"Several," Penny answered, "but they're called dry islands. The only water supply is from the rain."

"Then no one could stay there?" George asked.

"Not without coming here for water," Penny answered, her eyes going to the village side of the dock where there was a water spigot. She went over and turned it on. Water ran into the dry ground.

"So they'd need a boat to come and go," Nancy said.

"Do you think they took Bess to one of those islands?" George asked.

Penny shrugged. "She isn't here."

"Is there any way we can get there?" Nancy asked.

"Not without a boat," Penny answered.

"What about the little boats at the resort?" Nancy inquired.

Penny started to shake her head, then considered. "Well, on a real smooth day you could *probably* make the trip to Seahorse Island, and then it isn't far from there to Blue Cove. But unless you know the ocean and the islands real well, I wouldn't recommend it. I've been to both islands, but I wouldn't know how to get there now. My grandfather took me on the *Polka Dot*."

"Then there's no way we can go anywhere close to look for Bess?" George sounded as frustrated and angry as Nancy felt.

"Not without a big boat."

"What about the inter-island ferry?" Nancy asked, indicating the bill that she'd returned to Penny.

"It probably won't be back for several days," Penny answered, "and then only if whoever

114

took the supplies sent in an order for more goods to be delivered."

Nancy sighed. "I certainly hope we don't have to wait that long," she said.

"Well, do you want to search anymore?" Mr. Drew asked.

Nancy looked around sadly. "I don't think there's much use, do you?"

"Probably not," her father agreed and began trudging up the hill to the backbone of the island.

Nancy followed slowly, her mind considering the possibilities. If they could somehow find the *Polka Dot* or whatever boat had brought the intruders to the island . . . Or even get on board it long enough to use the radio. Her spirits lifted. There would be an opportunity, she was sure. It was just a matter of watching and being ready when the time came.

They were all hot and tired by the time they reached the resort, but a quick dip in the cove revived them enough for the girls to fix a light lunch. George sighed as she worked on the salad.

"I'm beginning to think you should have given that prize to Hannah," she told Nancy.

"We could use her help around here. I'm just not a super cook."

"Me neither," Penny spoke up. "My grandmother is terrific, but I've never cooked for anyone but myself."

"What we need is some fresh fish for dinner," Nancy suggested. "How is the fishing around here, Penny?"

"It's not too bad," Penny replied. "I used to go out in one of the little boats and just fish with a hand line. I couldn't supply all the guests, but I brought in three or four fish every time."

"Fishing in the cove?" Nancy asked.

Penny shook her head. "I caught some in the cove, but the best fishing is on the far side of the island. It's a long way to row, but you catch a lot more."

"Sounds like a good way to spend the afternoon," Nancy said.

"I'll envy you," her father spoke up from the sink where he was making lemonade from the supply of frozen juices. "I'm going to devote the afternoon to working on the radiophone. I don't know how much I can salvage, but maybe enough to build a simple transmitter—"

"Do you need an assistant?" George asked.

"I always liked jigsaw puzzles, and whoever hit that radio-phone sure created a dandy."

"That leaves us to do the fishing, Nancy," Penny said. "We can take both boats and try a couple of places, that way we'll be sure of catching something for supper."

"You'll have to tell me how a hand line works," Nancy told Penny.

"That's the easy part."

The conversation about fishing carried them through lunch, and afterward Nancy hurried to change to slacks and a cotton shirt that would protect her fair skin from the strong afternoon sun. She came out to find Penny waiting with lines, hooks, bait, and instructions.

"We'll row outside the cove," Penny said as they parted by the two small boats. "I'll go out around the cove and try to get to my favorite fishing spot on the far side of the island. You should stick closer to the entrance of the cove, all right?"

Nancy nodded, aware that it had been some time since she'd rowed a boat and a little apprehensive about taking such a frail craft out onto the bouncing waves of the ocean. "I think we'd both better be careful," she murmured. "After all, there's no one we can call for help."

Penny's smile faded a little, but she nodded without commenting. "If you get into any trouble with the boat, row for shore anywhere along the island," she told Nancy. "Even if you end up on the rocks, it doesn't matter. As Grandpa says, 'We can buy another boat'—just land safely."

The boats were surprisingly maneuverable in the gentle waters of the cove, and Nancy soon found her previously mastered rowing rhythm returning. Still, she didn't hurry after Penny when the other girl left the cove, preferring instead to enjoy the view of the resort and the surrounding gardens etched against the intensely blue sky above the snow-colored beach.

How can there be so much trouble here? Nancy asked herself as she directed the bow of the small boat toward the cove entrance and began to row more energetically.

The boat responded well till she hit the conflicting currents of the water beyond the cove, where it began to bounce rather frighteningly. Nancy slowed her pace and tried to choose a sheltered course, hesitant to venture far from the protective arm of land that kept the rough water outside the cove.

Now where did Penny tell me to fish? she mused, trying to remember what the redhead had told her. She let the boat drift for a few moments, resting her shoulders and the tender palms of her hands.

Every part of the island looked very much like the rest—the beacon tower of the resort was the only identifying landmark, and she had no idea where fish might be hiding. Finally, seeing that she was drifting away from the land, she simply put the oars to rest and baited the hook of the hand line, dropping it over the side without a great deal of enthusiasm. In her eagerness to catch fresh fish for dinner, she'd forgotten that fishing had its unpleasant moments as well as its exciting ones.

The first strike came quickly, and when she pulled the hook up, the fish on it was respectable both in size and type. "I must have found the right place," Nancy said out loud to herself as she put the fish in the small cooler and dropped her line over again. "I hope Penny is doing as well."

The second fish came along as quickly as did a third. The fourth fish, however, followed only after quite a wait in the hot sun. Once the fifth

fish was in the cooler, Nancy coiled the line in the bottom of the boat and stood up to stretch, her back and shoulders aching from her efforts.

A light breeze lifted her damp hair off her forehead, and as she looked around, a movement caught her eye. There was a boat just coming into view along the side of the island, and it looked very familiar to her.

Nancy sat down quickly and set her oars again, ready to row for the shore to get out of sight of the boat. Her oars dipped rhythmically, but her boat bounced erratically, and when she looked up, she realized that she wasn't making any headway against the tide.

A little chill of fear touched her spine and she began to row harder. The land stopped moving away from her, but it didn't grow any larger either, no matter how hard she tried. Her shoulders began to cramp and she had to stop rowing for a moment to ease them.

The boat was now much closer and Nancy was sure that it was the *Polka Dot*. Should she hail it? Ask for help? She looked around and felt surprised when she saw that land once more seemed to be approaching.

Then something else caught her attention—

cold water was washing over her feet! Nancy looked down and saw that the cooler was bubbing on water rising over the floorboards of the boat. She couldn't see the hole or whatever was allowing the water in, but it was obviously a large one, and the shore was still desperately far away! Nancy looked quickly toward the other boat, but it had disappeared! With no time to lose, she began to row with all her strength, praying that her rowing and the mysterious tide that was now carrying her would be enough to get her to shore.

14

Fearful Discovery

Nancy kept rowing, her lungs bursting from the effort, her eyes on the rising water level. If only there was someone else in the boat to help, to bail or try to stuff something in the hole. But she was alone.

The grating of the oars was loud in the muted world of her panting and the ocean's splashing wash. Her oar caught, jerking her painfully one way, then the boat bounced her the other and she sank into the water in the bottom of the boat for a moment before she regained her seat. Only then did she realize that she was aground!

For just a heartbeat, she let herself slump on the hard boat seat, easing the pain in her back and shoulders. Then she caught her breath and looked around. She was aground on the rocky shore somewhere below the ridge that formed the backbone of the island. From where she stood, she could see the bulge of the land that protected the cove, but the island curved enough at this point that she could see neither the entrance to the cove nor the resort above.

"Wow, that was close," Nancy muttered as she got to her shaky legs and stepped out of the boat onto the rocky shore. A couple of deep breaths and she turned her attention to lifting the cooler out and retrieving the hand line from the water in the bottom of the boat. Then she returned to the boat.

"Now, let's see just what happened," she said as she wrestled the heavy craft against the rocks and forced it over.

The hole was there—a small round hole so smooth that it was obviously not something that had happened accidentally. Nancy touched it and felt something sticky on her fingers, then looked into the boat, wondering if something had been plugged into the hole, something that had come loose while she rowed.

No plug was visible anywhere near the boat. Nancy sighed and tried to drag the boat higher on the shore, hoping to wedge it between the rocks strewn about the area.

Sighing, she looked up the steep hillside, knowing that she'd have an easier time getting back to the resort if she climbed up to the road. Then she remembered the big boat she'd seen. Where was it? She left the cooler and other equipment and moved out on the rocks.

The waves roared around her feet and the spray was salty on her lips as she leaned out, shading her eyes against the glare of the sun while she sought the outline of the boat she'd seen earlier. The waves washed the rocks on the hook of the cove and rolled through the opening, spending themselves on the sand.

Nancy frowned, then peered around again. There was nothing to be seen. No boat gleamed and bounced on the water, no distant motor sound reached her ears.

Could it be in the cove? Nancy hurried back to where she'd left her fish and fishing gear and picked up the cooler, aware that the fish would need to be cleaned and kept cold if they were to be dinner. It was a hard climb to the road with the extra weight of the cooler, but she made it. She hurried to the highest point of the road, and looked toward the cove between the palm trees that shaded her. A small boat was moving along near the hook of land that surrounded the cove. Penny was on her way home, too.

"Nancy?" Her father's voice brought her gaze back to the land, and she saw him approaching her at a fast clip. "What in the world are you doing here?" he demanded.

Nancy explained quickly as he relieved her of the cooler's weight.

"Do you think the plug was something that could be dissolved in salt water?" he asked when she finished.

She shrugged. "It sure seems as if it was intentional," she admitted. "I was just lucky that the tide caught the boat and helped me get to shore before it sank."

"What about Penny?" Mr. Drew asked.

"She's on her way in," Nancy answered. "I saw her from the road. There was something else, Dad," she said. "I saw the *Polka Dot.*"

"You what?"

"It was just before my boat started to leak," Nancy continued. "It looked like the *Polka Dot* was heading for the cove."

"Well, I'm sure it hasn't been in the cove," her father observed.

"How can you be sure?"

"We gave up on the radio-phone shortly after you and Penny left," he admitted. "Too much of it was totally smashed. We couldn't salvage anything, so George and I spent most of the afternoon on the beach. I changed and decided to walk along the road to see if I could spot you or one of the islands Penny mentioned."

"Did you?"

"It was too hazy to see the islands, and I didn't see any boat either."

"How long were you up here?" Nancy asked, frowning in confusion.

"Maybe half an hour before I saw you come scrambling over the ridge."

"Then you must have seen the boat," Nancy protested.

"Honey, I didn't."

Nancy looked up at her father, her brow furrowed, her lovely blue eyes troubled. She had seen it, she was sure. Yet the timing was such that her father had to have seen it, too, if it had sailed away from the island. And if it hadn't? There was no place it could have gone except into the cove—and she'd seen for herself that the water was empty.

"There's cold lemonade in the refrigerator,"

her father said as they neared the resort. "I'll clean the fish while you change into something a little less fishy."

Nancy smiled. "I guess I am a little ripe from the water in that boat," she admitted. "I think the last person to use it left their fish in the bottom instead of putting them in a cooler."

"I'm just very glad that you're safe. I want to look at that boat. Maybe Penny will know what was in the hole and why it disintegrated."

"I definitely want to look at it again, too," Nancy agreed.

The rear door of the resort opened, and George stepped out to greet them. "Nancy, what in the world happened to you?" she demanded.

Nancy repeated her story as she filled the tub with warm water. George shook her dark head. "I don't understand any of it," she admitted. "Why should anyone want to hurt you?"

Nancy shrugged. "I'm just glad it was the boat I took and not the one Penny has. She went a lot further than I did."

"Are you sure she's back?" George asked, instantly concerned.

"Dad and I saw her rowing into the cove just before we came inside," Nancy answered, dropping her fishy clothes in a pile.

"I'll go down and tell her what happened," George said.

"Ask her if she saw the *Polka Dot*," Nancy called after her friend, then stepped into the water with a sigh of contentment.

Penny was waiting in the lobby when Nancy emerged, dressed now in a pretty red and white print sundress. Penny's green eyes were worried as she scanned Nancy's face. "Are you really all right?" she asked.

"Fine now," Nancy said, "though I'll probably be a bit sore tomorrow from all the rowing."

"George told me what happened," Penny said. "You must have been terrified."

"I'm just glad it happened close enough to shore," Nancy admitted. "I really want you to see the hole in the bottom of that boat. It looks like it was done with a large drill."

"No one would patch a hole like that without being very careful," Penny murmured. "My grandfather takes care of his boats."

"How was your fishing trip?" Nancy asked immediately. "Did you catch anything?"

"Between us, we have enough fish for several days," Penny answered. "Your father insisted on cleaning mine, too, so I was just about to get things ready to cook them."

Nancy laughed. "I'm glad it's going to be

soon," she said. "I'm starving."

"I hope our lights are secure for tonight," Penny murmured.

"I guess they'll be all right if our visitors don't come back," Nancy observed, then asked Penny if she'd seen the big boat.

"It didn't come my way," the redhead answered. "I didn't see anything out there all afternoon. I was watching, too. Sometimes someone will sail by and I thought I could hail them and have them call for help."

Nancy shook her head in confusion as they went into the kitchen. George looked up from where she and Carson Drew were working at the sink. "Next time we fish and you two get to clean them," she announced with a grin.

"Speaking of next time, what about Nancy's boat, Penny?" Carson Drew asked. "Is there anything we can use to bring it back here to fix it?"

"The golf cart should be strong enough, shouldn't it?" Penny asked. "We don't have a car or anything like that. Heavy stuff usually goes on the *Polka Dot*."

"Do you think we could carry it up the hill to the road?" Nancy asked her father.

"It shouldn't be too heavy," her father said. "Shall we go now?"

"You've got plenty of time before dinner," Penny assured them. "The golf cart is in the shed over there, and the key is in it, I expect."

The trip along the road in the golf cart took only a few minutes, and Nancy stopped it just at the point where she'd come over the ridge to the road. "The boat is right down there," she said, pointing between two palms. "I remember that pink hibiscus. I think it's the only one along here."

Her father nodded, starting down the hill, slipping and sliding in the sandy soil. They were almost to the bottom before Nancy had a chance to look around. Her eyes went immediately to the rocks that had caught the boat as it washed ashore. The water level was different now, but the rocks were still well clear of the waves.

Nancy swallowed hard, staring at the rocky ground where she'd left the craft. "It's gone," she gasped, then bending low to study the ground, she pointed at the man's footprint that showed clearly in the damp earth. "Someone took my boat!"

15

Kidnapped!

Nancy and her father just looked at each other for several seconds. Then he sighed. "Well, I suppose it was someone from the *Polka Dot*," he said.

Nancy nodded. "Someone who didn't want us to know what they'd done to my boat."

Her father took her arm. "Let's get back and tell the others," he suggested.

There was little else to be done, though Nancy gave the half-hidden footprint another long look before she walked up the hill to the waiting golf cart. "Why would anyone take the *Polka Dot* to Florida and abandon it, then bring it back here?" she asked once they were underway.

Her father shrugged. "I've got a whole list of

questions to ask whoever is doing this," he admitted. "Starting with why they endangered you that way."

"And where they've taken Bess . . . and maybe the DeFoes," Nancy added.

"And why."

They both considered that for several minutes as they drove to the shed at the resort. "That's the most interesting question," Nancy observed. "I keep thinking that if we could just figure out why all these things have happened, we'd have a better idea of who is behind it."

"I just hope that Sheriff Boyd is getting very impatient to hear from us," Mr. Drew said, "so that he'll send someone to look for us."

"He's the type who just might send the Coast Guard." Nancy laughed.

"Well, what happened to the boat?" George asked, coming around the side of the shed. "Couldn't you carry it up to the road?"

"It's gone," Nancy answered. "Someone took it off the rocks where I left it."

"Probably the people on the *Polka Dot*," Carson Drew supplied.

"Then you think they were the ones who tampered with it in the first place?" George asked.

"If they were set on keeping us here on this

island, sabotaging the boats would be a good way to do it," Nancy admitted.

"But Penny's boat was all right," George reminded them both.

"I think we should make sure of that before anyone takes it out again," Mr. Drew stated.

"After dinner," George told them. "It's almost ready."

In spite of the difficulty of the day, dinner was a lively meal, and they were all in a good mood as they made their way down to the dock to inspect the single remaining boat. To everyone's surprise, it proved sound.

"Maybe they didn't have time to do both boats," George suggested.

"Or maybe they figured one sinking would be warning enough," Penny said.

"At least we're all safe," Mr. Drew reminded them. "And we're learning things about our adversaries, so that helps."

"I just wish we'd learn faster," Nancy murmured. "Fast enough to get Bess back."

"And my grandparents," Penny added, her usually bright face bleak for a moment. "I'm really afraid for them. They'd never let anyone take the *Polka Dot*."

"Isn't there any other way we could signal

someone?" Carson Drew asked after they reached the resort.

"I suppose we could try a signal fire," Penny suggested. "My grandfather told me that they used them a lot in the old days, before they had radios for communication.

"We'd have to build it on the other end of the island, because that's closest to Swallow Cay—the people there are the only ones likely to see a signal fire from this island," Penny explained. "Plus there are some people from the resort staff that live over there, so they'd be likely to want to investigate."

"Sounds good to me," Nancy said. "What do you say, Dad?"

"It's the best chance we've got at the moment, so I vote we give it a try."

"The same ridge can be seen from the dry islands," Penny warned.

"I rather hope someone there sees us and comes over to try to stop us," Carson Drew observed. "I'd like a chance to talk to them face-to-face for a change."

"Maybe we could find out what they want," George suggested.

"So what do we do?" Nancy asked Penny.

"Gather wood and clear a space on the highest point of the ridge," Penny answered. "At least that's what Grandpa says they did. I don't think he ever saw a signal fire here, but he told me so many stories." Her face softened and her eyes grew sad again, and Nancy knew that she was wondering if she'd ever see him again.

"I'm sure he'll be telling us some rare good stories once we find him and your grandmother," Carson Drew told her kindly. "Now where should we go to get the wood?"

"There's usually dead wood on the outer fringes of the island," Penny answered. "And there's a dead palm near the village, I saw it this morning."

"Well, if you've got an axe, I'll see what I can do with the palm," Mr. Drew offered. "The rest of you comb the beaches and clear the ridge. By dark we'll be ready."

This time Nancy welcomed the setting of the sun and the rush of tropical darkness that followed so swiftly. The pile of wood was large, and they had a second pile in reserve to keep the flames blazing as long as possible.

It was hot on the ridge, even with the evening breeze stirring the palms behind them. Nancy's shoulders ached both from the rowing and from the wood she'd carried to this spot.

"How long do you think we should wait to light it?" she asked.

"Till it's very dark," Penny replied.

George sighed. "I just hope the people who see it don't think we're having a gigantic wiener roast."

Penny giggled. "I think most of them would realize that a wiener roast would be held on the beach, not the high point of the island."

"I just hope there's someone watching," Mr. Drew murmured.

Nancy nodded, staring out over the dark sea, wondering where Swallow Cay and the other islands were, since she'd never been able to see any of them from here. It seemed an endless time till her father lit the huge pile of dry grass and leaves they'd gathered and placed at the heart of their woodpile.

The fire leaped to life with almost startling speed and the heat was more intense than any of them expected. They retreated at once, watching as the night breeze picked up a few sparks and spun them into the darkness.

"I hope we don't need these," Nancy said, tapping her foot against one of the pails of water they'd carried up from the village.

"It rained last night," Penny told her, "so everything is pretty wet in the brush. I don't think there's much danger as long as we don't have a lot of wind."

"Still, we'd better stay with this till it burns out," Carson Drew told them. "I'd hate to think we'd burned down the village or destroyed some of the brush with our signal fire."

George sighed, dropping to the ground and leaning against a palm. "I think I could sleep right here," she murmured.

"It's too warm for me," Nancy said. "I think I'll walk back along the road a little way. Perhaps I can see an answering fire or something else of importance."

"I expect they'd be more likely to set off a rocket gun," Penny told her. "That's what we'd do if we had the gun from the *Polka Dot*."

Nancy nodded and moved along the road, not hurrying. She wasn't really expecting to see a signal from another island. Mostly, she just wanted a few quiet moments to think. There was something nagging at the corner of her mind, if she could just remember what it was.

The pulsing sound of the motor didn't penetrate her concentration for several minutes, and by the time her ears picked it up, she was well away from the fire. Rescue? she asked herself, her heart leaping with hope. Or was it their enemies coming back to make more mischief?

Caution led her to the shadows on the edge of the road as she hurried toward the resort, aware that friends would land at the village dock, while their enemies would be much more likely to anchor in the cove and sneak up that way. Nancy smiled. If she could slip down to their boat while they were creeping up to the resort, she just might be able to get aboard and radio for help before they knew what was going on.

Suiting actions to her thoughts, she began running along the road, not paying any attention to anything but the area ahead, the break in the line of trees and bushes where the path from the dock came into view. She was concentrating so hard she didn't notice the shadow moving behind her—not until a hard hand closed over her mouth and a strong arm wrapped around her waist, bringing her to a sudden, frightening stop!

16

Timely Escape

"Just where do you think you're going?" an unfamiliar voice whispered in her ear.

Nancy tried to fight, kicking and struggling against the hold. But it did her little good, for she was dragged into the darkness and down the hill toward where she could hear the water lapping. The hand over her mouth kept her from crying for help and the difficulty in breathing made her dizzy.

"Who's that?" a second male voice asked as they stumbled to a halt.

"I think we might just have ourselves the elusive Miss Nancy Drew, Tom," the first man answered. "It was pretty dark up there, so we'll have to take her on board to make sure.

"Then what?" Tom asked.

"Well, it seems likely that her old man would be willing to trade the fancy gold necklace for her, don't you think?"

"Do you know how to use it, once we get it, Jack?" Tom's voice was familiar. Nancy recognized it as the voice of the "caretaker" she'd spoken with while she was still in Miami.

"I just know it's the key to the treasure, that's all." Jack's tone was grim.

"Think she knows anything?" Tom was staring at her in the light of the stars and the rising moon.

"Help me put her in the raft," Jack ordered. "I want to get her out of here before the rest of them miss her and come looking."

"What are they doing up there, anyway?" Tom inquired as they lifted her roughly into a bouncing rubber raft, then hauled it out into the waves.

Nancy tried to free her mouth again, but Jack's hold was firm and his thumb slipped up over her nose, cutting off all her air in warning. "The idiots are lighting a signal fire," he told Tom. "I guess they're getting desperate."

"Maybe we should let them get off the island," Tom suggested. "Get rid of them."

Jack freed her nose so she could breath, then laughed without humor. "Think they'll leave without the old couple and the blond girl?" he asked. "We let them contact anybody on the outside and this island will be covered with cops. We won't have a chance at the treasure."

"So what are you going to do?" Tom sounded dubious, as though he'd lost faith in the entire plan.

"I'll come up with a plan," Jack snapped. "You just be ready to help me once I get all the details worked out."

"I . . ." Tom began, but then the raft gave a strange jerk and Nancy felt the hold on her mouth and body released. The two men began swearing and moving around on the raft, nearly capsizing it.

Nancy didn't wait to discover what was causing the trouble. She rolled over the low side and into the cold water without hesitation, taking time only to glimpse the direction of the shore as she pushed off from the raft with one kick. Angry shouts filled the air as she stroked away, trying to keep as much of her body under the cool water as she could.

The splashing of oars sounded loud behind her, but she felt again the pull of the friendly tide that had helped her when her boat was sinking. This time she trusted the tide enough

to stop swimming and let it carry her along. In a moment she heard the words that told her she was doing the right thing.

"Where the heck did she go?" Jack was demanding.

"I don't see her," Tom answered. "Do you think she drowned?"

Muttered curses followed that suggestion and more splashing of oars as they moved the small raft one way, then another. Nancy lifted her head from the water to check her location and saw that she was drifting away from the bulk of the big boat, which appeared to be anchored in the lee of a large rocky ledge. The raft was now headed away from her and she was washing around the curving headland toward the cove.

Did she dare try to get on the boat? Nancy asked herself. She was swimming again now that she was sure the two men wouldn't easily spot her in the rough water. It was tempting. If she could just reach the radio and send an SOS . . .

"She must have gone under." Tom's voice carried well on the water.

"We'd better get out of here," Jack agreed. "They're going to come looking once they miss her at their bonfire. We sure don't want to be seen hanging around here."

Nancy stroked for shore, giving up any idea of trying to get on the boat ahead of the men. She had learned several things and she was anxious to discuss them with her father. If the men were leaving Anchor Island now, Nancy and the others would have the whole night to figure out what the medallion meant and to plan a way to rescue Bess and the DeFoes.

A sudden darkness overcame Nancy and startled her out of her thoughts. She paused, treading water as she looked around. She was no longer in the open ocean at all. Rocky walls rose on two sides with only a small ledge to offer her refuge as she tried to make sense of it.

"Well, for heaven's sake," she murmured as she pulled herself up on the ledge, shivering with the effect of the cold water and her brush with the kidnappers. From the ledge she could see the rocky slit that she had come through and she realized that she was in some kind of cavern.

Though she was curious about it, the velvet darkness was close to complete—so deep she couldn't even see how far the cavern continued into the island. Sighing, she scrambled to her feet and tried picking her way along the rough ledge toward the starlit world outside.

After a few feet, she was forced back into the

deep and restless water, which was hard swimming until she was clear of the opening. Her strength was nearly gone by the time she pulled herself up onto the rocks and lay there panting, cold and miserable, but glad to be safe and free of the men.

"Nancy, Nancy, where are you?" George's voice echoed strangely down the hillside.

"George!" she shouted. "George, I'm down here!"

The welcome finger of light from a flashlight sliced through the darkness around her, and in a moment George came sliding down in a shower of rocks and sand. "What in the world happened to you?" she demanded as soon as she saw Nancy's dripping, bedraggled condition.

Nancy explained as quickly as she could while George helped her climb the hill to the road. "What are you doing here?" Nancy asked, looking back along the road to where the fire should have been blazing. "Where is everyone? What happened to the fire?"

"I was looking for you," George answered, then continued taking Nancy's questions in order. "Your father and Penny are down in the village keeping a watch for sparks. We had to douse the fire when the wind suddenly shifted. I guess you didn't notice it on the water, but Penny says it's a storm wind and it does seem to be blowing harder."

Nancy shivered as they left the protection of the trees and brush, and she felt the strengthening wind as it blew from a new direction. "That could have been bad," she agreed. "With the fire, I mean. Did anything burn?"

"We had to put out a couple of grass fires and one roof got a little singed, but Penny found a hose to attach to the faucet in the village, so they have everything under control there. They'll just have to wait till they're sure nothing more is smoldering."

"Dad must be awful worried about me," Nancy said, hesitating, torn between a need for dry clothes and the knowledge that she should go and let her father know she was safe.

"You go in and get into dry clothes," George ordered, seeming to read her mind. "I'll go tell your father what happened. We'll be back as soon as everything is watered down."

"Thanks, George," Nancy said. "That wind is really cold with wet clothes."

George chuckled. "It felt good to us while we were up by the signal fire, but I'm beginning to see what Penny means. It does feel colder and damper now. I think it is bringing in a storm."

"I'll make some cocoa as soon as I get dry," Nancy promised, leaving her friend and running in her squishing sandals, which she'd never had time to remove. Luckily, she'd come ashore close to the resort, so the distance wasn't far.

The lights were burning in the kitchen, telling her that Tom and Jack hadn't bothered with the generator on this visit, which was a relief. What had they been doing here? she asked herself as she stripped off the ruined shoes and padded barefoot and still dripping through the resort to her room.

A quick hot shower rinsed the salt water from her hair and skin. She wrapped her hair in a towel and pulled on a warm pants suit, then hurried to the kitchen to put the milk on to heat for the cocoa. That started, she opened the freezer and took out the bread loaf that contained the medallion.

The icy gold necklace gleamed at her tantalizingly as she unwrapped it. The key to the treasure—that was what the men had called it. That seemed to fit with the legends Penny had told them. Yet what did it mean?

Nancy held the medallion in her hand, her fingers covering the side that had been damaged as she stared at the rest. It looked like an anchor, she realized suddenly. A current of excitement burned through her as she set the medallion on the table and studied it, comparing it to an image in her mind. She was still there when the kitchen door opened and the others trooped in.

"What is it, Nancy," her father asked, his tone heavy with concern.

Nancy looked up at him, her face blazing with joy. "I think I know what the medallion means," she told them. "I've discovered its secret!"

17

Exploring for Answers

Penny moved to the stove to stir the cocoa as Mr. Drew and George joined Nancy in bending over the medallion. "Don't you see it?" Nancy asked as their curious gazes left the medallion and returned to her face.

"I guess not," her father admitted. "What is it?"

"A broken anchor," Nancy answered. "Just as this island is in the shape of a broken anchor."

"That's true," Penny said, joining them. "I think that was the first name for the island, but it got shortened to just plain Anchor Island."

"You mean the medallion wasn't damaged?" Carson Drew asked, picking up the necklace to study it more closely. "Then what is all this gold work on the other side?" His fingers traced the lines that had been etched into the disk.

"I think it's a map," Nancy answered. "A treasure map!"

"The pirate treasure?" Penny gasped. "You mean all the legends are true?"

"Well, that's what Tom and Jack seemed to think," Nancy answered. "That's why they're keeping us here. They seem sure that the treasure is somewhere on this island and that this medallion is the key."

"Those scratches are impossible to read," George said. "They don't make any sense."

Nancy nodded. "Precisely what I was thinking. So why don't we try to get a clear rubbing of them with paper and soft lead or charcoal."

"I've got some charcoal," Penny said. "I brought all my art supplies. I even have some paper that should be just right for a rubbing on something that fine."

"Suppose you fill me in on the details of what happened to you, Nancy," Carson Drew suggested as Penny left the kitchen, while George poured the cocoa and got some cookies out of the cookie jar.

Nancy recounted her kidnapping and escape

as fully as she could, describing the men in limited detail, but enough so that George nodded. "That's the Tom that met us, all right," she said. "But he was alone on the boat, I'm sure."

Nancy sighed. "I expect Jack was still in Florida somewhere with the *Polka Dot*. I still don't understand why it was taken there, then brought back here. But I am sure that it was the boat I saw tonight and this afternoon."

"But where could it have disappeared to so quickly?" George asked, remembering what Nancy had told her. "Surely one of us would have seen it if it was chugging around the island."

"I've been thinking about that," Nancy admitted, "and I wonder if it could have been hidden in that cavern."

"The one where you were tonight?" George frowned.

"What cavern?" Penny asked as she came in with the art supplies.

Nancy explained as the redhead began work on the medallion.

"I don't remember any cavern," Penny said, frowning at her first rubbing and trying a second with a slightly different technique.

Nancy described the opening and the area as

well as she could, but there was no spark of recognition in the green eyes. A third and a fourth rubbing were done as they all watched. Finally Penny straightened up and handed the fifth one to Nancy. "I think that's the best I can get," she said.

"Don't you know anything about the cavern?" George asked Penny.

"I remember a kind of small opening along there, but nothing big enough for even a rowboat except at low tide," Penny replied, then smiled. "Of course, it could have opened up during some of the storms. My grandparents wrote that there were a lot of cliff cave-ins after the big storm they had this spring. Maybe it was a large cavern with a very small entrance till the outer rock face broke away."

Nancy nodded. "We'll have to go down there tomorrow and look. I'm sure it's wide enough for a boat, and the water was deep, too. When I slid off the ledge, I couldn't touch bottom. I had to swim back out."

"Do you have any idea what these lines could mean, Penny?" Carson Drew asked, turning the rubbing first one way, then another.

"They don't look like any paths I've ever seen," Penny answered, sipping her cocoa and taking one of the cookies they'd thawed out that morning. "In fact, the only areas of the island wide enough to have paths like that are right here at the resort and the village area. The rest of it is just long and skinny."

Nancy picked up the tiny squiggling mass of marks and compared them to the broken anchor in the medallion. There was a tiny upside down V on the anchor, and after a moment, she saw the same mark in the midst of the rubbing. Matching one to the other, she compared them and felt her heartbeat quicken.

"It's the cavern!" she shouted. "It has to be the cavern."

"What has to be the cavern?" Mr. Drew asked, setting his cup down and bending over the tracing and the disk with her.

"This," Nancy answered, indicating what looked like a tiny equal sign on one side of the rubbing. "See how the lines seem to radiate from that point?"

"You think this is a map of caverns under the resort?" Carson Drew gasped, following her thinking at once.

Nancy nodded, then looked at Penny. "Could it be?" she asked.

"A lot of these islands are honeycombed with caves and caverns," she began, "but I—"

A loud crash stopped them all. Nancy looked around, suddenly afraid that the men had returned and might now be coming to take the medallion and the secret she'd just discovered. However, the racket continued and Penny quickly identified it as a shutter blowing in the wind.

"I think we should close the shutters over the small windows," she said. "This is going to be a bad storm."

"I'll help you," George said before Nancy could offer. "You keep looking at that map, Nancy. Maybe you can find some more clues."

"What's this?" Mr. Drew asked, using a pencil tip to indicate another equal sign on the opposite side of the marks.

"Another entrance?" Nancy gasped. "But where?"

They studied the map in silence for several seconds, comparing it to the broken anchor design of the medallion and their own rather sketchy mental maps of the island. "As near as I can figure, it should be somewhere near the generator building," her father said after several minutes.

Penny and George came in, smoothing down their hair and smiling. "Everything is secure for the moment," George reported, "but that's

155

not saying how long the wind will leave it that way. We were even thinking of boarding up the big windows to protect them."

"Penny, do you know of any caves in the area near the generator building?" Nancy asked, her mind on the puzzle, not the approaching storm.

"The Singing Rocks," Penny answered at once. "I used to love them when the wind was right, but my grandparents wouldn't let me spend much time over there. They said the caves were dangerous."

"Do you think we could go look?" Nancy asked.

"Now?" Penny gasped.

Nancy nodded, not sure why she suddenly felt a sense of urgency. There was something about the caverns, something more important than the treasure, yet she had no idea what it was. "I really think we should," was all she could say.

"We'll need flashlights and maybe a lantern," her father said, looking skeptical.

Penny brought flashlights for everyone and two lanterns, matches, and even a ball of twine. "We can use this to leave a trail," she explained. "I have a friend who is into exploring caves and he always does that so he can find his way back out."

"Beats a trail of bread crumbs," George quipped as they let themselves out into the wind-torn night and followed Penny along the road to the small hump that was the generator building.

Finding the entrance of the cave proved difficult. Nancy sensed that the others thought she was behaving foolishly, but something kept her from postponing the search till morning. Something told her to keep looking, to go into the maze that must spread beneath the lovely hill on which the resort had been built.

"Here we go," Penny shouted at last, her words snatched away by the wet wind that harassed them seemingly from every side. "This is the biggest cave, I think. Anyway, it's the only one I've been in. Hear the singing?"

Nancy gasped as the whistling and humming filled the air around her. It was a sad sound, lost and lonely, speaking of storms and abandonment; yet it was beautiful, too. She could almost imagine people being haunted by the wind's music.

"Now what?" George asked as they moved well back in the cave, out of the wind and away from the fullest swell of its singing.

Nancy took the rubbing from her pocket and trained the flashlight's beam on it. "If we're here," she began, tracing the spiraling lines with her fingernail, "this line seems to lead toward the deepest tangle of caves or tunnels."

"Don't forget the twine," Mr. Drew counseled. "I don't really want to be lost down here tonight, not with that storm blowing in."

"I'll tie the end around that," Penny agreed, pointing to a small pillar of stone that rose from the cave floor to a height of about two feet.

Nancy started along the cavern, finding it fairly easy going since the ceiling was high and the floor relatively smooth. She tried to match the curves and turns of the rocky hollow with those on the medallion, but the light was too poor, and as they moved deeper, there were other openings off the main tunnel.

"Do you think this goes clear down to the cavern you were in?" George asked after what seemed a long period of silence.

"I wish I knew," Nancy admitted.

"We're going to have to stop pretty soon," Penny called from her place at the rear of the group. "My string is almost gone."

"Oh, no," Nancy muttered, her sense of urgency growing rather than lessening as she moved through the narrowing tunnel. The walls were growing damp now and the ground was somewhat slippery beneath her feet, yet she was sure that something important waited just ahead.

"That's it," Penny called.

"I really think we should turn back," Carson Drew said. "We can leave the string in place and bring more tomorrow. That way we can explore the side tunnels and—"

Nancy clutched his arm, stopping his words as a distant sound reached her ears.

"What is it, Nancy?" he whispered.

Nancy listened, waiting for it to come again, but the silence was broken only by the dripping of the seeping walls.

"Did you hear something?" George asked, coming forward to join Nancy and her father. "What was it?"

Nancy looked at them, her eyes wide with anxiety. "I think I heard a call for help!"

18

Rescue in the Caves

In the silence that followed her words, the sound came again. For a heartbeat she thought it might be the singing sounds they'd heard at the entrance, but it wasn't. This was a human wail of despair and it wasn't far ahead!

"You stay here, Penny," Mr. Drew called. "At least where you can see the end of the string and guide us back in case we have to pass any side tunnels."

Nancy plunged down the tunnel, shouting, "We're coming! Keep calling!"

The echoes of her words were confusing, but once they'd died away, she heard voices again, this time more than one, and louder, much

160

louder. She followed the sound as best she could, passing two side tunnels, then turning to the left when the cavern split.

The search ended abruptly as she came to an ancient heavy, metal-banded, wooden door that blocked an opening in the side of the continuing passage. The sounds came from behind it and Nancy had no trouble recognizing one of the voices.

"Bess," she called. "Are you all right?"

"Nancy, oh, Nancy, get us out, please. Please hurry before we drown!" Bess's voice was high with terror.

"We're opening the door," Carson Drew assured her as he put his shoulder to the heavy wooden bar that secured the door. The dampness had made the dry wood swell and it was hard to lift it, but with Nancy and George adding their strength to his, it finally popped free of the metal brackets that had held it.

The door burst open and Nancy screamed as icy water swept over her, nearly washing her down the passageway. As it was, she held out her arms and caught a stumbling figure, pulling an older woman out of the rushing flood. Two more figures were caught by Mr. Drew and

George, after which the racing water subsided to a light flow that barely reached the tops of their shoes.

"Who . . .?" Nancy began, and then her mind supplied the answer. "Mrs. DeFoe?" she asked.

The slightly haggard face was instantly split by a warm smile. "You must be Nancy Drew," she said. "Bess told us that you'd find us, but I'm afraid we were beginning to lose faith."

"Oh, Nancy, we would have drowned in another hour," Bess wailed from her cousin George's arms. "The water started coming in from the walls and the roof and it couldn't get out around the door, so it got deeper and deeper and . . ." She dissolved into tears again.

"She's right, young lady," the man said. "We couldn't have lasted much longer. But how in the world did you find us? I've lived on this island a good bit of my life and I didn't know this area existed."

"We'll explain everything when we get you safely back to the resort," Mr. Drew told them. "Right now we'd better get back to Penny. She must be frantic."

The climb back out of the system of tunnels proved to be much quicker than the exploration had been. Penny's joy at finding her grand-parents alive and safe made Nancy feel even better, though her mind was spinning with questions.

When they reached the upper cavern, they all stopped, shocked by what had happened. The wind no longer sang through the hollowed areas of rock: it now roared and screamed in frustration, driving great sheets of rain against the headland of the island.

"So that's why the water was pouring in," Mr. DeFoe murmured. "With this much wind the waves must be very high—and it's raining hard, too."

"Who put you in there, Grandpa?" Penny asked. "How long have you been there?"

"Since just a few days after we closed," he replied. "We were getting ready for your visit when two young men stopped by. They seemed nice enough, so we invited them to have lunch. They were interested in the history of the islands."

"They seemed awfully interested in our plans for the summer," Mrs. DeFoe continued, shivering even though she was sandwiched between her husband and Penny. "That made me suspicious. They didn't like it when I told them that we were expecting guests."

There was a moment of silence, and then Mrs. DeFoe looked at Nancy. "I guess I should apologize for having tricked you into coming here," she said with a gentle smile, "but at this moment, I'm just glad you did."

Nancy laughed. "Then the contest prize was just to tempt us to come?" she asked.

Mr. DeFoe nodded. "I suppose I could've called you just as easily, but I wasn't sure you'd come right away, being such a busy young lady. I figured you wouldn't be too busy to refuse a contest prize."

"We'd read so much about all the cases you and your father had solved," Mr. DeFoe continued, "so we thought . . . well, we thought if you came to the island and heard all the legends about the pirate treasure, you might be interested in looking for it."

Mrs. DeFoe sighed. "Of course it's too late now. The young men will take it all as soon as the storm is over. There's no way to stop them, since they did something to one of the rowboats to keep you on the island. They told us that."

"Have they found the treasure?" Nancy asked.

"I don't know," Mr. DeFoe admitted. "All they said when they brought our food tonight was that they might never have to come back again except to let us out. I don't think they'd give up without having found the treasure, not after all they've done."

"I don't think they have any idea where to look," George said, then described Nancy's brush with Tom and Jack.

"You have the medallion?" Mrs. DeFoe gasped, looking up at Nancy.

"Right here," Nancy admitted, producing it from her pocket. "That's really how we found you." She showed them the rubbing that Penny had made from the medallion and explained how the necklace had come into her possession.

"Do you think we can make it back to the resort?" Carson Drew asked. "You three need dry clothes and some proper rest before we talk any further."

"I'm sorry, you must be exhausted," Nancy agreed, feeling guilty about all the questions that still filled her mind.

"I think we should wait a little longer," Mr. DeFoe replied, moving forward to study the violent scene beyond the cave mouth. "Storms this strong usually have small breaks between the squalls. This one has been going on long enough to be weakening soon."

"Where did you get the medallion?" Penny

asked her grandparents as they all moved to the rear of the cave and settled along the wall. "I never saw it before."

"I found it," Mr. DeFoe answered. "The last big storm rearranged quite a lot of the land. It broke off the cliffs, tore out trees, and generally stirred things around. So I was checking the coast from one of the small boats when I realized that the storm had opened a cavern. I went in to look around and found this lying on a ledge."

"We showed it to a few people," Mrs. DeFoe continued the recital, "and they all said they thought it might be the one in the pirate legend. That's when I got the idea of asking Nancy Drew to help us discover what it meant."

"Only the thieves got here first," Penny finished for them.

Mrs. DeFoe nodded. "They made me write that note for you, then took us on the *Polka Dot*. We spent a couple of nights on Seahorse Island, but they were afraid some fisherman might come by and see us, so they brought us over here and shut us in that horrible tunnel." She shuddered.

"How long have you been there?" Carson Drew asked.

The Defoes shrugged. "It seemed like forever," Mr. DeFoe replied, "but I doubt that it was more than a day or two before Bess joined us."

"How did that happen, Bess?" George asked. "I didn't even know you were missing till after Nancy and Mr. Drew arrived."

"I was walking on the beach, and I saw the boat," Bess said, speaking calmly for the first time since the rescue. "I didn't think much about it till I recognized Tom on the deck. I guess they were afraid that I'd tell someone because they came over and offered to take me to see the cliff grotto. I thought it would be fun." Her pretty face showed that it had been a far from pleasant experience.

"I thought it might be something like that," Nancy said.

"I was sure you'd find us, Nancy," Bess continued, "but when the water started to pour in, I was afraid that you wouldn't be in time." Tears welled up in her eyes.

"Don't think about that now," George counseled.

Nancy started to ask a question, then stopped as she realized that the howling of the wind had eased a little and the pounding of the rain had almost stopped. "It sounds like the storm is breaking up," she said, moving at once to the cave entrance.

Mr. DeFoe came with her, the wind ruffling his gray hair as he peered out at the lashing trees, more visible now that the clouds were being blown away. "I think you're right, Nancy," he said. "This could be the best time for us to go."

"Lead me to a tub of hot water and a decent meal," Bess groaned as she scrambled to join them. "For that I'll brave any storm."

"We'll make a run for it." Mr. DeFoe moved back to take his wife's arm, gesturing for Penny to take her other hand. "Let's all hold on to each other," he suggested. "It's not going to be an easy climb up to the road."

His words proved prophetic, and after what seemed an eternity of scrambling up the soaked hillside, they were all moving along the mud-slick roadway toward the resort. The wind buffetted them roughly, and the misty end of the storm plastered their hair and clothes to their bodies as they strained toward the welcoming bulk of the building. They were all panting from exertion when they reached the kitchen.

They dropped into chairs at the table, gasping, but Nancy went on through the swinging doors into the dining room and crossed to the big windows with their view of the cove. She was drawn there by the panorama of the sky as the storm clouds surrounded the moon. But as she looked out, she gulped in shock. Moonlight glinted on the *Polka Dot* as it drifted aimlessly on the wind-whipped waves!

19

Smart Decoy

Nancy watched the boat for several minutes, unaware that her clothes were dripping a puddle of water onto the floor at her feet. It was still blowing wildly outside, and the boat staggered about the cove like an abandoned creature. Nancy stared at it, trying to see if it was being guided. Suddenly a warm hand touched her shoulder. She jumped.

"What are you doing in here, honey?" her father asked.

Instead of answering, Nancy pointed to the cove.

"The *Polka Dot*," he gasped.

"I think it's been abandoned," Nancy said. "At least no one seems to be on the bridge, and it isn't anchored or anything."

"Maybe they tied it up at the dock and it got loose," Mr. Drew suggested.

"Then where are Jack and Tom?" Nancy asked.

Their eyes met for a moment, and then they went to the kitchen. The others were just getting ready to go change to dry clothes. Penny had put a pan of stuffed chicken breasts into the oven to cook, since her grandparents and Bess had nearly starved on the short rations Jack and Tom had supplied. Everyone stopped talking when the Drews entered, their faces making it clear that they sensed that something was wrong.

Mr. Drew cleared his throat. "I think you should know that the *Polka Dot* is derelict in the cove."

"And the men?" Mrs. DeFoe gasped.

"We don't know," Nancy admitted, "but they must be somewhere on the island."

"We should try to get the boat," Mr. DeFoe said. "If we could all get on board and get away from here, then we could radio for help."

"There's no way we can get to it," Nancy told him. "The only small boat is kindling under the dock or else sunk. I was looking for it after I saw the *Polka Dot*."

"I guess there's nothing much that can be done at the moment," Mr. Drew said, "except keep an eye on the boat. If it gets close enough to shore, maybe we can go down and try to get on it."

Mr. DeFoe sighed. "The way things have been going, the next squall will either drive it out of the cove or put it on the rocks."

"If it runs up on the beach, we could still use the radio," Penny reminded him.

"In the meantime, I think we'd all better change into dry clothes," Mr. Drew said.

Nancy laughed, breaking the tension. "If this keeps up, I'm going to run out of clothes," she announced. "I've done nothing but put on dry clothes all day long."

"We probably should all just go to bed," George observed. "Do you realize it's the middle of the night?"

They all looked at each other. Then Bess stated, "I'm not sleepy, I'm hungry."

"I don't think any of us will be able to sleep while those men are out there somewhere," Mrs. DeFoe remarked, sobering them.

"Perhaps we should check and make sure that no one has gotten into this building, Mr. Drew," Mr. DeFoe suggested.

The two men left, and Nancy went back to the window, watching as the boat plunged about the cove, battered by the waves and harried by the wind that drove it first one way, then another. Slowly, the scene dimmed as the rain clouds returned and the wind sounds changed again. Nancy was glad when her father came to tell them that they'd found no sign of intruders.

"They must be holed up somewhere else," Nancy said. "No one would stay out in this storm."

"The food will be ready in about forty-five minutes," Penny announced, returning from the kitchen. "Think we can be dried off by then?"

Nancy changed her clothes adding a light sweater that felt good as the wet wind forced its way through the resort building's cracks and chilled the air. She was exhausted, yet her mind refused to stop.

The lines of the rubbing map moved through her mind like a tangle of string. Was there truly a treasure hidden at the end of one of the tunnels marked on it? But if so, why hadn't Tom and Jack found it, since they obviously knew their way through the maze well enough to use it as a prison?

And where were they? That question chilled her more than the weather. When she went out to the lobby, she found Mr. DeFoe at the window, staring at the blackness beyond. "Where do you think Tom and Jack are?" she asked him.

He shrugged. "Probably in one of the cabins."

"Why would they come here in the storm?" Nancy asked. It was a question that had bothered her while she changed.

"They wouldn't have much choice," he replied. "Seahorse Island has no good anchorage for the boat, and with the water as high as it is tonight, the island might even be underwater. It's a low, flat kind of island. It loses half its area to high tide or this kind of sea." He sighed. "I'm just glad they brought us over here when they did—and glad that you found us when you did. We would have as little chance of survival in that tunnel as we would have on Seahorse Island."

As the others joined them, more details of what had happened were discussed, and Nancy began to feel that much of the mystery had been explained—all except the most important part. No one had any idea where the pirate treasure might be hidden.

"Tom and Jack don't know either," Bess informed Nancy as they leaned back in their chairs, full of food and sleepy. "They were arguing while we were on the boat. Tom kept telling Jack that his map was a fake, that they'd explored the whole system of tunnels and there wasn't any treasure."

"But they stayed to look more," George reminded her.

"Jack said there was something that went with the map, some kind of key; but he didn't know what it was."

"The medallion," Nancy supplied.

"But what does it mean?" Mrs. DeFoe asked.

Nancy shook her head. "I can't seem to figure it out," she admitted.

"I think we all need some sleep," Mr. Drew suggested. "Let's barricade the doors and go to bed. Maybe things will look better in the morning."

Since they were all too tired to argue, they left the table as it was and stumbled off to their beds, well aware that dawn was not too far away.

In spite of the late hour, Nancy slept poorly and woke early. The silence that greeted her was almost eerie after the night of howling wind and pounding rain. Nancy got out of bed and pulled on her clothes before padding to her glass door to look out. The scene was almost mockingly tranquil. Sun spilled over the dripping world, and the distant ocean sparkled as the waves danced. Only when she looked closely could she see the broken palm fronds on the ground, the torn bushes, the battered and bruised blossoms drooping from hibiscus bushes.

Suddenly, there was a flash of movement off to her left, and Nancy gasped as she saw Jack stepping out of the dark shadows near the closest cabin. A moment later, Tom joined him and the two of them moved toward the path to the beach.

Nancy slipped from her room and ran to the dining room, her eyes scanning the beach and the cove, seeking the *Polka Dot*. The boat was there, all right, beached clumsily on the far side, the waves lapping lazily at it.

The radio! She remembered only too clearly what had happened to the radio-phone in the resort and she had no doubt that they would do the same thing to the one on the boat, especially now that they knew they were all trapped on the island because of the storm-beached boat.

"Nancy?" George came around the corner as

she was moving the barricade from in front of the door. "What's going on?"

"Get Dad and tell him that Tom and Jack are going after the boat," Nancy called. "I'm going to try to stop them." She opened the door and ran out into the cool freshness of the morning, ignoring the questions that George called after her.

Once on the path to the beach, she realized that there was little she could do to stop the two men. She had no weapons, nothing to threaten them with. She slowed down and peered ahead, seeking the young men, not sure what she was going to do.

They were already on the beach, moving away from her, heading toward the boat just as she'd feared. Nancy hesitated, then made her decision. George would bring her father and the others to her rescue. For now, she had to decoy Tom and Jack away from the boat, so she picked up a rock and threw it against a nearby clump of storm debris. As she'd hoped, it began to slide down the hill noisily and the men looked back at her.

Nancy gave them a moment, then ran the rest of the way to the beach and started away from them through the sand toward the inland swell of land that marked the opening between the cove and the sea. For one horrible moment, she was afraid the men wouldn't follow her, but then she heard the sound of their slipping and sliding progress as they loped along the beach after her.

"Where is she headed?" Tom asked, his voice carrying in the silence.

"Doesn't matter," Jack panted back. "She's the one to trade for the necklace."

Nancy looked up, ready to turn toward the resort so that her father and George could come to her aid, but the way was blocked by a storm-toppled palm. For the first time, fear swept over her as she realized she couldn't double back—the men were too close. She had trapped herself!

The beach turned to rocks and the land fell away as restless waves came crashing through the opening, carrying with them snags of wood and other flotsam from the storm. Nancy hesitated, then began to climb, feeling the touch of the wind as she left the protected cove and started up the steep cliff face.

"We've got her now!" Jack shouted, his tone filling her with terror as the rock and sand began to shift beneath her feet, making her slide backward instead of letting her get above the men. Her fingers and toes were scraped and bleeding as she continued to scramble against the unstable ground, seeking something to cling to, something to pull her up away from her pursuers.

20

Treasured Solution

"That's far enough!" Her father's voice came clearly on the air, and Nancy heard two yelps of surprise from Jack and Tom.

She stopped fighting the shifting ground and allowed herself to slide back toward the beach, not daring to look over her shoulder till her feet were resting on a stable rock. When she did, she burst out laughing.

For a moment Carson Drew's face stayed grim, then he, too, began to laugh, as did George and Mr. DeFoe. The axe gleamed brightly in the morning sun as Mr. Drew lowered it to the sand. "It was the only weapon I could find," he admitted. "You didn't give us much warning, Nancy."

"I was just afraid they'd get to the boat and wreck the radio," Nancy told him as Penny came panting up with a coil of rope.

"What now?" Mr. DeFoe asked after Nancy and George tied the hands of the two bearded and weary-looking young men.

"Is there some place we can lock them up?" Mr. Drew asked Mr. DeFoe.

"The root cellar should do," Mr. DeFoe answered promptly. "It's not too big, but it has a nice stout door and I have a good padlock for it."

"That ought to take care of them," Carson said, sounding pleased. "If Penny can show us where it is, why don't you go on around to the boat and see if you can reach the authorities, Jeff. There must be a lot of people wondering about all of us by now."

Mr. DeFoe nodded, looking none the worse for the ordeal he and his wife had been through. "I'm just glad to see the *Polka Dot* again," he said. "I was afraid something would happen to it when they said they were going to use it to leave a false trail in Florida."

"Why did you bring it back?" Nancy asked the glowering men. "Why didn't you leave it there?"

"Tom's boat was too small for the treasure," Jack answered sullenly. "I figured we'd need it."

"Do you know where the treasure is?" Penny asked.

For a moment Jack just sneered at her, but Tom laughed bitterly. "He doesn't know anything," he taunted. "He has a map, but all we found were the caverns. There's nothing in there. Someone got that treasure a long time ago."

"It's got to be there," Jack protested. "We just didn't have enough time to search. We found the ocean entrance, didn't we? And all the caves." He turned his glare to Mrs. DeFoe, who, along with Bess, had come down to investigate. "Why didn't you and the mister leave the island like everybody else?" he demanded. "You brought all this trouble on yourselves by hanging around here."

"Let's put you in the root cellar," Mr. Drew said, tugging on the rope. "Then we'll have an expert do the looking." He winked at Nancy.

The next hour was one of busy confusion as the men were locked away and a hasty breakfast was prepared. Mr. DeFoe came in to report that he'd reached a rescue boat in the area and that the authorities would arrive before evening. He also brought the faded, ancient map that had led Jack and Tom to Anchor Island.

"Well, Nancy, I guess it's up to you," Mr. Drew said as they spread the map on a nearby table along with the medallion and the waterstained rubbing of the map on it. "What do you make of it?"

Nancy studied the map, seeing for the first time how much the island did resemble a broken anchor. She traced the coast and noted the water opening that she'd found herself in when she escaped from the men earlier.

"Their map doesn't show the other entrance," she murmured. "And there's not too much indication of the tunnels we saw last night."

She moved the rubbing closer and began to compare the two, gradually forming in her mind a picture of the passages. There were a number of them, more than she remembered seeing as they'd explored before they found Bess and the DeFoes.

"I think we'll have to go back into the caverns," she said, looking up. "There's something here in the center that I don't understand."

Preparations took only a short time, and the day was warm and sunny as they all trooped along the drying road toward the cave entrance. The twine still lay as they'd left it and they lost no time in moving through the narrow and twisting passages.

When they reached the end of the twine, Penny tied on a new ball and they continued down the damp passage, relieved to find that water no longer poured into it from the leaky prison where Bess and the DeFoes had been confined. There were more side tunnels, but each was disappointingly empty.

Then, suddenly, they were at the bottom. The ocean lapped at their feet and they could see the distant light where the passage opened to the sea.

"Where is it?" Bess wailed. "Nancy, where is the treasure?"

"Could we have missed it in one of those tunnels?" Penny asked.

The others said nothing, but Nancy could see that they, too, were disappointed. She took out the medallion and studied it in the flickering light of the lanterns and flashlights. There *was* something . . .

Afraid of raising their hopes falsely, Nancy

moved away from them as they poked around the lower passage. She climbed slowly past the first side tunnels, then paused at the door they'd opened the night before.

She could find the tiny marks on the map that seemed to indicate the prison passage. The odd marks she couldn't decipher were on the other side of the main passage line. The beam of her flashlight was weakening, but she slowly moved it over the seemingly solid face of the rock wall, not sure what she was seeking.

Even with extra care, she almost missed it. The years and the wearing of the dripping water had taken their toll of the chipped-in niche.

Heart pounding, Nancy reached into the hollow, her fingers grasping the lever it concealed. She pulled it, not sure what to expect.

The click echoed in the cavern stillness. A section of the wall seemed to shift and swell like a wave. Then it turned, and the beam of her flashlight touched the darkness beyond and lit it with the gleaming of gold.

Nancy opened her mouth, but no sound came out. Fortunately, George had come up to find her and she quickly called the others. Hesi-

186

tantly, they all stepped around the balanced boulder that had swung aside and entered the treasure chamber.

Trunks, cases, and jeweled caskets were stacked everywhere, as were bars of gold bullion and rotted sacks of gold coins. Golden utensils gleamed when the dirt was brushed away. It was nearly an hour before any of them even thought of leaving the chamber.

"Do you think we should just leave it here?" Bess asked, reluctantly placing a lovely emerald necklace back in the dark-wood-and-gold casket. "It's all so beautiful."

Nancy laughed. "It's been safe here for hundreds of years," she reminded her friend. "I don't think anyone will find it while we have lunch and wait for the authorities to come and take Jack and Tom away."

"I can hardly wait to tell them that you found it," Mrs. DeFoe said with a smile. "That will let them know just how stupid they were."

"I was lucky, too," Nancy reminded her. "We had the medallion and that was the final clue."

"It wouldn't have done them any good, anyway," Bess stated firmly. "They couldn't have figured it out the way you did."

Nancy blushed as the others all agreed with the evaluation. Though she loved mysteries, she was frequently embarrassed by people's comments after she solved them. "So what are you going to do about the treasure now that we've found it?" she asked, to change the subject.

"I'm sure the Historical Society people will be anxious to see it and catalogue it before it's removed from the cavern," Mr. DeFoe replied. "In fact, once we get full radio contact set up, I think I'll see if most of our staff would like to work this summer. I'm sure we'll be running at nearly full capacity once the story gets out."

"More than full," Mrs. DeFoe agreed. "But I'd like to have the staff start right away—that is, if the four of you will stay on as our guests?" Her eyes twinkled in the light of the lanterns, and her smile was wide as she added, "I can't promise you as much excitement as you've had so far, but if you'd like to enjoy the beach and the fishing and exploring the treasure room, you are more than welcome."

It was only a brief pang of regret that Nancy felt as she realized her island detective work had come to an end. Her next mystery, *The Silver Cobweb*, would be just as exciting.

She sought her father's eyes for permission to accept the DeFoes' invitation and was delighted when he nodded. Bess and George quickly added their agreement, hugging Nancy as they all made their way out to the welcoming sunlight.

You are invited to join

THE OFFICIAL NANCY DREW ®/ HARDY BOYS ® FAN CLUB!

Be the first in your neighborhood to find out about the newest adventures of Nancy, Frank, and Joe in the **Nancy Drew** ®/ **Hardy Boys** ® **Mystery Reporter,** and to receive your official membership card. Just send your name, age, address, and zip code on a postcard *only* to:

The Official Nancy Drew ®/
Hardy Boys ® **Fan Club**
Wanderer Books
Simon & Schuster Building
1230 Avenue of the Americas
New York, New York 10020

OFFER VALID ONLY IN THE UNITED STATES.

NANCY DREW MYSTERY STORIES®
by Carolyn Keene

The Triple Hoax (#57)
The Flying Saucer Mystery (#58)
The Secret in the Old Lace (#59)
The Greek Symbol Mystery (#60)
The Swami's Ring (#61)
The Kachina Doll Mystery (#62)
The Twin Dilemma (#63)
Captive Witness (#64)
Mystery of the Winged Lion (#65)
Race Against Time (#66)
The Sinister Omen (#67)
The Elusive Heiress (#68)
Clue in the Ancient Disguise (#69)
The Broken Anchor (#70)
The Silver Cobweb (#71)

You will also enjoy

THE LINDA CRAIG® SERIES
by Ann Sheldon

The Palomino Mystery (#1)
The Clue on the Desert Trail (#2)
The Secret of Rancho del Sol (#3)
The Mystery of Horseshoe Canyon (#4)
The Mystery in Mexico (#5)
The Ghost Town Treasure (#6)
The Haunted Valley (#7)
Secret of the Old Sleigh (#8)